One Night Surrender

Book #3 in the ONS series

Katelyn Taylor

Copyright

Trigger Warning

Please carefully review these triggers before continuing. This book is forbidden by nature with a complicated and somewhat taboo relationship between a woman and her adopted brother. The triggers inside this book include but are not limited to:
Adopted siblings, ass play, spanking, kidnapping, violence, graphic sexual scenes, graphic language and more.

Dedication

Keeping it in the family has a whole new meaning with this one.

Chapter One
Naomi

You know that friend in the group who's always deemed the shy one? The safe one? The one you mercilessly tease for being too innocent or sheltered? The one you would never expect to step a toe out of line, ever? Yeah, that's me.

Arianna gives that black-cat energy with her laid-back I very clearly have mommy and dead daddy issues but don't let it bother me attitude, while Cassi is our hyper-crazy, mildly inappropriate best friend who balances out Ari's moods. Then there's me. The quiet one, the shy one. The virgin. A title my best friends never let me forget.

It's not like I haven't been propositioned. I mean, I'm twenty-one, a junior in college. I could've slept with hundreds of guys and girls by now if I wanted to. It just never felt... right. I never had a problem with being a virgin; it didn't seem like something that was necessary to give away to the first taker. No judgment to others, I've just always been... content, I guess.

So when Cassi announced that for her twenty-first birthday she wanted to visit a sex club and I finally agreed to go, her jaw hit the floor. Arianna was shocked too. I wasn't going to not celebrate one of my best friends' birthdays just because the venue was a little out of my comfort zone. I also couldn't deny there was a small spark of curiosity inside me, but now we're standing on some sketchy side street looking up at a blank, unassuming building, I'm suddenly filled with a rush of nerves.

An imposing man slips out of a door, and Cassi tosses her red hair to the side and smiles up at him like she's ready to seduce her way past him if that's what it takes.

"Gratify," she practically purrs.

The man nods and gestures towards our masks. "Masks on, ladies, and welcome to paradise."

My stomach flips at his words as I quickly tie the red mask against my face. It's a bold contrast against my bright blonde hair and black dress, but Ari and Cass both said it looked amazing, so I'm rolling with it.

Slowly, we make our way through a dark hallway. It goes on for so long that, for a moment, I panic. Did Cassi walk us straight into some kind of trafficking trap or something? Honestly, she has been known to act first and think later. I tried to research this place to find out if it was reputable, but the website was mysterious and extremely vague. I'm sure it's an anonymity thing for their clients, but still, something about this whole thing is rubbing me the wrong way. I don't like this. I don't like it at all. We should—

Before I can even finish that thought, a whole new world practically opens up before us. Lights are flashing, music is thumping, and people are, well, fucking. Everywhere. It's not like some gross darkened basement where you just see flesh on flesh. Instead, it's glittering diamonds around necks, sexy lingerie, little black dresses and... tits.

My eyes lock on to a woman riding a man on a couch in the center of the room. She's facing us, and with each thrust, her tits bounce, entrancing me.

"Fuck," I mutter before I can help it.

Just because I'm a virgin, doesn't mean I haven't explored my sexuality, especially in the safety of my bedroom. My laptop is armed with the best antivirus equipment money can buy, which leaves me free to indulge in my fantasies until my heart is content and my vibrator is dead.

It didn't take me long to realize it wasn't about men or women specifically. Everyone is beautiful, but I'm attracted to people who intrigue me, who interest me, regardless of gender or orientation. Though I tend to lean towards men, I could never and would never deny the sight of a beautiful woman. Especially one that looks like her.

I drink in the sight, and the woman's gaze meets mine before a seductive smile spreads across her face. I can feel myself flush under her watchful eyes, and I instantly look anywhere but at her. Fuck, I don't think I can do this. I'm not ready for this kind of pressure. I'm awkward as fuck. I can't flirt; I'm not smooth. I'm that extremely sheltered girl who only had one boyfriend in high school, and he ended up breaking up with me after three dates when I wouldn't fuck him in his mom's SUV after school. I dated a few guys extremely casually but only got to dry-humping with one my freshman year. That's it—the total of my sexual experiences lives and dies with Brad Williams. Honestly, it's humiliating.

"I told you guys, right?" Cassi cries as she bounces on her toes. "I wonder where the bondage demonstrations are."

Ari looks less intrigued than us; instead, her hesitation is heavy as she assesses the room while Cassi leads us to a staircase on our left. I pause for a moment before hurrying after her, my curiosity getting the better of me.

When we get to the top of the stairs, we find a man standing there with an iPad in his hand.

He smiles. "Welcome. What desires can we fulfill for you today?"

"Are you on the menu?" Cassi shamelessly flirts.

He's a good sport—he gives her a patient smile and shakes his head. "Unfortunately not, but two beauties like you should have no trouble finding company for the night. Do you have any rooms, kinks or demonstrations you're interested in? We have sensory deprivation rooms, exhibitionism/voyeurism displays, group play, bondage—"

"Bondage! Definitely bondage," Cassi squeals.

He smiles politely as he gestures towards a set of elevators. "Next floor up, second door on your right."

"Thank you!" She grins.

"What kind of sensory deprivation rooms do you have?" I say shyly. "Or, like, what are they?"

God, Nay. Could you sound any more pathetic?

Thankfully, the man is kind and doesn't make me feel like a total inexperienced idiot.

"We have a dark room where anyone can step inside and be immersed in the moment. We also have an array of toys to take away senses, as well as a glory-hole room and—"

"Glory holes? That's a thing?" I ask quickly, though even I notice there's more curiosity in my tone than anything else.

"Oh, very much so. They're pleasurable for both parties, a certain anonymity where you can just... be," the man says.

I can feel Cassi's rounded eyes on me as I slowly turn my gaze to her. She isn't judging by any means, but I still feel a level of embarrassment for sure.

"The glory-hole room is just down this hall to your left," the man intervenes, gesturing behind himself.

"Meet you back at the hotel?" Cassi asks me with a knowing smirk.

I struggle to meet her gaze for a moment, feeling more than a little embarrassed before I nod quickly and hurry down the hallway. I don't honestly know where I'm going, and I don't really care. I just want away from Cassi's shit-eating grin.

Once I turn a corner, the hall grows darker, only soft red lighting leading the way. There are several closed doors either side of me, and

I can faintly hear the sounds of whips, chains, and both deep and soft moans drifting through them.

My feet carry me to an open gallery of sorts. Two men are passionately fucking in one room while a group of onlookers watch through a glass wall. An exhibition room? I pause for a moment, entranced by how they embrace each other so fervently, how their eyes frequently drift to the crowd before their tempo increases, like the audience is fueling their performance.

After they both reach their release—alongside some of the audience members who've, um, taken matters into their own hands—I continue wandering through the club. I'm honestly a little dazed and more than a little out of my depth. It feels as if I've been drop-kicked straight into one of the pornos I watch late at night, only I'm unsure I want to participate. I'm unsure I want to be here. I mean, I don't have the confidence of Cassi or even Ari. I can't march myself right into a bondage demonstration or sleep with a total stranger on a whim.

Couldn't you, though? What better night to push the boundaries of your limits than here, right?

Nodding to myself, as if forcing myself to summon some courage, I turn and see a plaque outside a door that reads *Dark Room.*

Curiously, I move towards it. The attendant standing outside it offers me a welcoming smile.

"If you'd like to engage, move to the center of the room. If you need a break, move to the perimeter. The exit signs will be the only thing lit in the room, and you can take your leave at any time. If you feel unsafe at any time, you need only call out 'gratify' and one of our roaming security guards will quickly intervene. Step through this door and the next to enter the dark room."

I'm blown away with the level of security precautions they're taking to ensure the mental and physical safety of their customers. I don't know why I expected this place to be some sweaty, crowded orgy—it's clearly anything but. The velvet walls, marble floors and polished metal railings everywhere should have given that much away.

I nod to acknowledge the man's instructions, then he opens the door and gestures for me to step inside. Hesitantly, I take a few steps forward, and then I'm plunged into total darkness. For a moment, I panic. I've never been afraid of the dark by any means, but nerves like I've never experienced before are racing through my body. Blindly, I reach out in front of me before feeling a door handle. This must be the one he mentioned.

You can do this, Nay. If you don't like it, you can move on. You can do this.

After that little mental pep talk, I push the door open and step forward. At least, I think I'm stepping forward. I see nothing for several feet, until I look up and spot the faint red glow of an exit sign across the way.

I stand there for a moment, my eyes rendered useless—but that means my ears begin to pick up on everything. Soft moans and sighs, lips meeting lips, whispered words being met. Someone bumps into me, and it jars me for a moment before I feel the wall behind me. Remembering the man's words, I slowly move to the center of the room. Or at least what seems like the center of the room. Awkwardly, I bump into one person before stepping on another's foot. They grumble at me as I apologize. Fuck, this was a mistake.

Then a soft hand reaches for mine before trailing up my arm to my neck. It's slim, gentle, and when a soft pair of lips just barely brushes the corner of my mouth, I know it's a woman.

Heat pulses through me as she adjusts her aim, moving to the center of my mouth before her soft lips pull at mine. I find myself sinking into the kiss, not knowing where to put my hands for a moment before resting them on what I think are her hips. Silky hair caresses my fingertips as I do. Holy shit, is her hair really that long? I start playing with the ends of it, and she breaks our kiss and moans into my ear.

"Fuck, I love my hair being played with."

Her voice is pure sex, and I don't have any words to reply before her mouth is back on mine, her tongue twirling around my own as I tentatively run my hands up her back before sinking them deeper into her hair.

She moans into my mouth, almost like a reward, so I tug on her hair, earning yet another moan. I feel drunk on her mouth, like I could stay like this for the rest of time. God, maybe I lean to men way less than I thought because kissing a man has never felt like this.

The woman has positioned herself so she's grinding herself against my leg. I can feel her pussy growing wet, only a pair of panties separating her and my bare leg as she uses me for her pleasure.

Someone comes up behind me then, a pair of lips latching on to my neck as what feels like a beard scratches the sensitive skin there.

"I could hear you moaning all the way across the room," a man rumbles into my neck.

For a moment, I think he's talking to me, but then the woman pulls her mouth away from me and speaks.

"She tastes like fucking heaven. See?"

She wraps her hand around my jaw, forcing my head backward before a new pair of lips meets mine. The kiss is so intensely different, it sends my head spinning. The man takes full advantage of the kiss, pushing his tongue into my mouth in a much more aggressive way than the woman did. It's still pleasant, and the entire moment is exhilarating, but I have to admit, I'm not enjoying him as much as I did her.

"Fuck," he rumbles. "Might have to take her back to a private room for some fun, Star."

The woman in front of me laughs, still grinding her pussy on me as her hand wanders up my leg and beneath my dress. Her finger traces the line of my panties. "What do you say, princess?"

Excitement and hesitation fill me in equal measures, and my mouth opens and closes like I'm a fish out of water. But I'm silent a moment too long it seems because, as one, the man releases his hold on me, the woman removes her hand and they both take a step back.

"No worries. We're moving to room fourteen if you change your mind," she says, pressing a soft kiss to the corner of my mouth once more before slipping away.

I'm left reeling in the middle of the room when another stray hand touches my ass. For some reason, the allure of the moment is suddenly gone, and I find myself wanting to get out.

I move towards the wall the best I can and keep my hand on it as I head towards the exit sign. When I finally make it through the door, something like relief washes through me, and I find another man standing guard outside. He gives me a polite nod, and I nod in response as I all but stumble down the hall.

I pass by a mirror and pause to take in my reflection. What looks like black lipstick is smeared all over my face, and there's a red mark on my neck that looks like a mixture between a hickey and a scratch from the man's beard.

I do my best to wipe the black lipstick from my face then continue down the hall. Wow. That was... something. It was overwhelming and overstimulating but oddly empowering and exhilarating. Though I'm not sure I loved the idea of so many people having access to me at once, I can't deny that the anonymity that room provided gave my confidence a boost I didn't know was possible.

I'm walking a little taller, with a little swagger in my hips almost. It's unlike me in every way, shape and form, but I kinda like it.

Chapter Two
Naomi

As I'm moving through the club, another wall plaque catches my attention.

Glory Hole Hall.

I hesitate only for a moment before I open the corresponding door and find a worker standing there, one hallway to his left and one to his right.

He smiles at me politely. "Welcome. Will you be giving or receiving tonight?"

My mind goes blank for a moment. "Um, like sex or... other stuff?" I ask, hating how unsure I sound.

He nods like he understands completely. "The limits are set by you and your consenting partner. If you would like to offer, say, oral, you only need to rest your mouth at the start of your designated hole. You're able to communicate between the wall should your desires change."

I swallow and nod. "I'd like to try giving... oral, that is... um, please?"

Fuck. Shoot me in the goddamn face. Could I be any more cringe?

"Right this way then," he says, gesturing towards the left hallway. "Number six. Enjoy."

"Thanks, you too," I say and hurry off down the hallway.

Then I pause. You too? Christ on a corndog, Nay.

Shaking my head, I continue down the corridor before rounding a corner to find a line of doors, almost all of them closed except for the one with a six on the door. Carefully, I step inside and shut the door behind me. There's a light in the ceiling, nice maroon walls surrounding me and a fluffy white carpet beneath me. I also see several stools, benches and pads for... well, comfort, I suppose?

Of course, the most obvious part of the room is the hole in the wall. Probably six inches in diameter, though I expected it to be bigger. I mean, I know some people fuck through these things. How would that even work?

Turning my head to the side, I slowly lift one leg up and scoot closer to the wall, simulating what you'd need to do just to get your pussy close enough for penetration. Unfortunately for me, my balance isn't the best in flat shoes, let alone stilettos, and I go down hard.

I land on the floor with a hard thud. "Shit."

"You okay over there?" a man's voice calls through the wall.

Embarrassment hits me, and I can feel my cheeks heat as I scramble to my feet. "Y-Yeah, yes. I'm fine."

"Cool, get to sucking then," he says before I hear the sound of a zipper and he pushes his cock through the hole.

I wrinkle my nose in distaste. At his words and, frankly, his dick. I've seen plenty of cocks in porn, none in real life, but that's beside the point. I've seen enough to know that they shouldn't look like... that.

Still, this is part of the experience... I guess.

Slowly, I sink to my knees, his semi-flaccid cock mere inches from my mouth.

There's a groan of frustration from the other side of the wall. "I don't have all goddamn night."

Before I can even snap back at him, he's almost ripped away from the wall, his voice rising to a shout before a door slams shut. Some banging occurs on the door before a new cock is pushed through the hole.

I hesitate for a moment as I look at it. Long, thick and fucking tattooed. Swear to God, from base to the start of the tip, it's completely inked up. I've never seen anything like it. The tattoos are like decorations on what I can only assume is the prettiest cock that's ever existed.

I wait for him to be an asshole too, to be impatient. Instead, he just stands there, silent and waiting, almost as if he's telling me he has all the time in the world.

That thought helps a bit.

Nervously licking my lips, I study the cock as I try to recall every blowjob scene I've ever watched, every story Ari and Cassi have ever told me. Every horror memory I've unfortunately heard my older brothers talk about. I guess the bright side to this is that if I'm terrible, I never have to see the guy again.

I open my mouth before leaning forward and slowly closing it around the tip. A choppy breath is released on the other side, and I think that means I'm doing good. I carefully push forward, taking more of his cock into my mouth—inch by inch until he reaches the back of my throat and I gag. Awesome.

Embarrassment rises inside me before another satisfied groan rumbles from the man on the other side of the wall, spurring me on. I withdraw before pushing forward again, stopping just before I gag. This time, I run my tongue up the side of his cock, and I hear what sounds like his fist hitting the wall, like he's having to brace himself.

Smiling against his cock and so fucking relived I'm not completely messing this up, I do it again and again. Pushing myself deeper each time, licking him for longer. My confidence grows with each bob of my head, and when I wrap my hand around his base to assist, the loudest groan yet escapes him.

"Fuck," he mutters, though it's barely audible.

I try different techniques, running my tongue under him, around in a circle, even gently grazing my teeth along the side. He seemed to like that one most of all.

It's hard to fully wrap my head around the fact that this person is a literal stranger. I've never met him, I've never even seen him, yet here I am sucking on his cock like it's my favorite popsicle and I'm desperate for his taste.

His cock twitches in my mouth as his thrusts through the hole increase. They come so quick I'm barely able to keep rhythm, and then suddenly he pauses. His cock throbs in my mouth and a warm, thick liquid hits my tongue. It's surprising at first, and for a moment, I freeze. Then my mind fully grasps that he's coming.

Swallowing him down as best I'm able, I continue my movements, putting more effort into the actual swallowing part as he groans.

"Fuck, Peaches!"

I freeze at his words.

What. The. Fuck?

"What did you just call me?" I ask shakily, to which he doesn't respond.

Instantly, it's like a bomb has gone off. My vision is distorted and my hearing is dulled, just a quiet ringing in my ears as I shakily rise to my feet and run. I don't know where I think that'll get me, but I run, and I don't fucking look back.

I make it to the hallway and am almost to the exit when I slam into a hard body. Instantly, the smell of leather, whisky, and something inherently him hits my senses. I know it's him before I even look up. I can *feel* it.

Still, my eyes need to confirm what my brain already knows.

Slowly, I lift my gaze, meeting those deep blue eyes that have plagued my every thought for as long as I can remember.

Kolter Mayhew.

My adopted brother.

Chapter Three
Naomi

Nick and Kolter are on the couch playing video games while Mom works a shift at the diner down the road. She's been working a lot lately, which means most days I'm home with Nick and Kolter, since Anthony is now in college. Nick and Anthony are my older brothers, and Kolter, I guess technically, is too.

His dad was sent to jail a few years ago, and my mom took him in. Being Nick's best friend, he was practically living here anyway, and as of last month, Kolter legally became a part of our family. A brother. My brother.

I've been mildly in love with my brother's best friend as far back as I can remember and fought against him becoming part of the family, though no one knows why. I've done a good job of keeping my crush a secret over the years, but I find it harder and harder the older we get. I know there is an age gap but that doesn't matter to me, and I don't think it matters to him either. I swear, sometimes when I'm not paying much attention, I'll find him already watching me. Kinda like how I watch him when he isn't looking. I think he secretly likes me back. Or at least I hope he does. Now that he's technically family, though, it's weird... right?

"Nay! Bring us some snacks," Nick calls out from the living room.

I frown at his attitude before opening the fridge and the freezer. I consider the options before pulling out some pizza rolls. They could eat like a thousand of them in a day, no lie.

I dump them onto a plate, put it into the microwave and start the timer before making my own afternoon treat. Once I'm done, I carry the plate and my bowl to the living room and set it down on the table.

Nick shoves a pizza roll into his mouth then immediately starts panting. They're still scalding.

"That's what you get for not having manners," Kolter teases before looking to me with a kind smile. "Thanks, Nay."

My heart flutters at his use of my nickname as I scoop up a spoonful of my own treat and take a bite. I groan in happiness and go to scoop up another spoonful when Kolter leans over.

"Whatcha got there?"

I blink. How embarrassing would it be if I spat food at him while trying to talk?

"Peaches and vanilla ice cream," I say as clearly and carefully as I'm able, though it doesn't sound all that clear since my mouth is numbing further with every passing moment.

"Fucking gross," Nick sneers.

Kolter bumps his shoulder into his. "Language."

Nick rolls his eyes and refocuses his attention on the video game while I pout in defense.

"You've never even tried it! It's really good! Do you want to try some, Kolter?" I ask, unable to hide the hope in my voice.

It's like, if he likes the snack I created, then maybe it's the first step in him liking me? How dumb does that sound?

Kolter looks down at the contents of the bowl for a moment like he's weighing the risks before he gives me a short nod. I rise to grab him a new spoon, but before I can, he reaches over and takes mine, gathering up a nice portion before lifting the spoon to his mouth.

I watch his lips close around it. I know I'm being a weirdo by *watching him so closely, but I can't help it. He grabbed my spoon—he used my spoon! His mouth is right where mine used to be. Nothing can convince me he doesn't feel the same way now. I'm practically planning our wedding in my head as we speak.*

He gives me a thoughtful nod as he swallows the treat before handing the spoon back to me. "Not bad, Peaches."

Peaches. A way better nickname than Nay. And even better, he came up with it on his own, for me.

I'm already plotting how I can get him to say it again. Maybe I can record him saying it, so I never have to stop hearing it.

"Peaches," Kolter says as he looks down at me.

His hands are currently gripping my arms, steadying me. They tense in a way that's almost painful before he slightly loosens his hold. Wow. He looks so... different. He sounds different.

I haven't seen Kolter in a little over six years, though we stopped being close long before that. He's grown taller since I saw him, he has a beard now, and his thick black hair is almost to his shoulders. That hair is pushed back from his face, revealing the tattoos that crawl from his hands to his neck. Paired with his black combat boots, dark jeans and black cut-off leather jacket, he looks every bit intimidating as I know he is. Every bit as dangerous. The eyes don't lie, though. They're the same beautiful blue ones I stared into all my childhood; that I dreamed of. His black mask can't disguise them—I'd recognize those eyes in every lifetime.

He was twenty the last time I saw him, and even though that's well into adulthood, those six years have transformed Kolter Mayhew completely. He's no longer the broken boy with a soft spot for me. This Kolter Mayhew is all man, and if the way he's looking at me is anything to go by, I'd say that soft spot is long gone, hardened to stone.

"K-Kolter?" I breathe roughly, still unable to believe he's actually right in front of me.

Am I drunk? I don't think I am. Come to think of it, I haven't had a sip of anything since getting to the club.

"In the flesh. What's the matter? You look surprised. This is what you came for, right?"

"What? I... Huh?" I stammer like a complete idiot.

His expression twists into a sneer as he shakes his head. "Tongue-tied? Just a few moments ago, you were putting that thing to good use."

The harshness in his tone catches me by surprise. I know we grew apart as we got older. His dad got out of prison, he stopped coming home for dinner as often, started hanging out at his dad's bar... and then he was just kinda gone. According to Nick, he joined his dad's motorcycle gang and has been riding that outlaw life ever since. Mom doesn't approve but still invites him home for every holiday and birthday. He always declines. Apparently, he rarely even sees Nick. Maybe once or twice a year max.

"I didn't know it was you," I say, blushing as I look down at my feet.

One of his hands releases my arm, forcing my face up so I meet his gaze.

"Nope, you were just getting on your knees for any cock that pushed its way through that hole, huh?" he snarls. "Gotta say, never pictured little Nay to be the whore type."

His words hurt, like he's stabbed me in the chest, and I shake my head, trying to throw off his accusations.

He scoffs and releases me with a rough shove. "Get the fuck outta my sight."

I stumble for a moment before finding my balance. Then a man with a matching leather cut-off comes swaggering over, swinging his arm around Kolter's shoulders.

"Well, well, well. Who do we have here, Blade?"

"Blade?" I echo as I look between the men.

The guy's eyes stay on me, running over me in a way that sends a shiver down my spine. It makes me feel exposed, dirty, and I immediately decide I don't like him at all.

Kolter's eyes stay on mine, his stony expression never wavering for a moment.

"No one. She's no one."

Chapter Four
Kolter

Those big grey eyes stare up at me with an overwhelming amount of hurt before she scurries away. Good. Little priss like her doesn't belong in a place like this.

"What was that about?" Ace asks.

I look over my shoulder at him and wonder what Naomi thought of him. She doesn't know anyone from the gang besides me, and it's been years since I've seen her. I'm not that same kid she used to know. Not even fucking close.

I shake my head and run a hand through my hair. "Nothing. I'm out of here. See you back at the clubhouse."

Before he can question me or insist that I stay, I'm gone. I do my best to conceal my wandering gaze as best as I can while I weave my way through the club, but once I catch sight of a soft swish of bright blonde hair ducking out around the corner, I know I'm headed in the right direction.

She heads down the main staircase, looking a little turned around for a moment until she finds the exit. Looks like it was her first time tonight. I wonder what else she got up to.

Running into her was unexpected. I turned the corner and saw her coming out of the Dark Room, curiosity got the best of me and now, after wondering my whole damn life, I finally know what her mouth feels like.

It was disappointing at best.

I keep a healthy distance between us, so she's none the wiser that I'm trailing a hundred feet or so behind her. She makes her way through the hallway to the main street, and when she steps through the door, I pause, allowing her time to figure out her ride or whatever.

After a few seconds, I push through the door and find that she hasn't made it far. She's only just ahead, on foot.

My jaw tenses as irritation pulses through me. I just wanted to make sure she left the club; now I'm gonna have to make sure she doesn't get goddamn jumped because she's too fucking naïve to understand how rough this area can be, especially at night.

She wraps her arms around herself as if that will protect her from the biting night air. Hate to break it to her, but she'd be better off in a pair of panties and a T-shirt than that dress. My cock twitches in my pants at the thought of that, and I blow out a frustrated breath as I head for my bike.

I don't start it up until she's almost completely out of my sight. And when she *is* fully out of my sight, I take off towards her.

Hours pass as I watch her aimlessly wander the streets, like she doesn't have a place to go back to. Or maybe she doesn't want to go back. It's not until the sun is just starting to come up that she finally heads towards a hotel, practically limping inside. I'm sure walking the streets in high heels for hours has to hurt like a bitch.

The entire time I followed her, she didn't look over her shoulder once. She's so fucking unaware of the world around her. Just like when she was a child. The kid hasn't even changed one goddamn bit.

Well, maybe a little bit.

As soon as she scans her room key against the locked entrance and steps through, I rev my throttle and take off down the road. Fucking finally.

I should have gone home hours ago. I should have given up on being her shadow for the night. Old habits die hard and all that, I guess. For months after I left the house, I'd follow her around. I knew Nick didn't pay enough attention to her, and with me out of the picture, she was at risk. Don't ask me why I fucking cared back then.

I merge onto the highway then pick up speed, cranking the throttle as I weave in and out of the early-morning traffic. My eyes are burning with exhaustion. I've been up for thirty-two hours, and I can fucking feel it too.

I didn't want to go out tonight. I almost didn't. A bunch of the guys are regulars at that place and wouldn't stop fucking bugging me to come out with them. I finally caved just to shut them the fuck up. Now I'm fully realizing what a fuck-up that was because not only am I deadass tired, but I also now have those stupid fucking grey eyes practically burned into my head. Eyes I've worked very hard to forget.

Her grey eyes look up at me, her lower lip jutting out. Goddamn. Is she able to make them bigger when she wants something? Christ, it's like two oceans looking up at me, pleading with me. She makes it so damn hard to say no to her.

Something I never do.

Except tonight. Tonight is a hell fucking no, and she needs to understand that no matter how many tricks she pulls, I'm not caving. Not this time.

"Kol, please," she asks, the soft lilt of her voice tugging at my chest.

If only she knew how wrapped around her finger I am. It would be the end of both of us, for sure.

"Peaches, I said no."

She frowns at that, crossing her arms like a petulant child, not a fifteen-year-old who's on the honor roll, the captain of the debate team, a prize-winning chess player, and a closet sculpture artist. I couldn't even name a sculpture artist to compare her to. It would be useless because they don't hold a fucking candle to her anyway. She's brilliant and kind and soft and beautiful...

"C'mon, you've never let me ride your bike. You take all the hussies around town on it but not me. Am I not good enough?"

I laugh at that and shake my head, pinching her chin between my thumb and forefinger. "Hussies? What are you, a seventy-nine-year-old woman?"

"I'm serious," she whines.

My tone takes on a level of seriousness I didn't plan as I lower my gaze to hers. "Peaches, it's dangerous. They don't matter; you do."

Her pupils flare, the way they always do when I give her this level of attention. She wants me, the same way I want her. I've known it for a while now. She's probably wanted me for even longer, though I don't see how that's possible.

Naomi runs her tongue against her bottom lip, wetting it like she's preparing herself. It fucking pains me, and every fiber of my being is ready to say to hell with everything and taste her lips once and for all. Fortunately or unfortunately, one of the prime reminders of why I can never have her comes bouncing into the room. and I release her chin with a rough jerk.

Nick's eyes bounce between us for a moment before he smirks. "Kolter, you gotta tell me when we're roughing up Nay so I can help!" he says and wraps her up in a headlock, rubbing his knuckles against the top of her scalp.

"Nick! Darn it! Stop it!"

Nick laughs. "Ooooh, darn it. You hear that, bro? Our little sister has quite the potty mouth."

Nick is my best friend and technically my brother, but that doesn't mean I've ever looked at Naomi like a sister. Not once.

Figuring this is my best way to escape, I grab my keys and wallet and shove them into my jacket as I head for the door.

"*Wait, where are you going?*" *Nick asks, slightly out of breath before releasing a pissed-off Naomi.*

"*Out,*" *I say over my shoulder.*

Nick frowns. "With your dad?"

I give him a rough nod, and what looks like disappointment crosses his face.

"*Man, since he got out of prison, I never see you anymore. We were supposed to go to college together, chase tail all over this town; instead, he's got you working crazy hours, and for what?"*

Nick isn't judging—he just doesn't understand. His dad bailed before Naomi was born, so he doesn't get why I would want anything to do with a father who was absent from my life for so long. I wish I could explain to him that I go out of necessity, not loyalty; that my dad is a crazy fucker, especially when he doesn't get his way, and this is safer for all of us.

"*I'll be back as soon as I can,*" *I say to him, though my eyes are heavily on Naomi.*

She looks more upset about my leaving than Nick, and I hate to admit that I really fucking like it.

Before I know it, I'm parking in front of the clubhouse. Shaking my head, I look around the empty street and wipe a hand down my face. Reminiscing about the past while I'm driving? I need some goddamn sleep.

Chapter Five
Naomi

It's the early hours of dawn when I walk into our hotel room. Cassi thought it would be fun to rent one for her birthday, and it is convenient because despite me being twenty-one, my mom still likes to know where I am and who I spend my time with every second of the day.

I'm as quiet as possible, but as soon as the door shuts behind me, Cassi and Arianna both sit up, their eyes slightly sleepy but on me.

"Are you just getting in?" Arianna asks.

"Sluttt," Cassi teases.

I try to muster a smile as I shrug. With every step I take, I limp a little more, so the moment I kick my monstrous heels off is cause for celebration. Never again.

Arianna frowns down at my feet. "You didn't walk here, did you?"

"No, um, the guy I spent time with gave me a ride. He was nice."

Except he wasn't. He was the opposite of nice. He was a jerk, he was mean, he was vile.

"Shut the fuck up. How nice was he exactly, Nay? Can we finally tear up your V-card?" Cassi asks. "You know the best birthday present you could ever give me is finally having sex?"

"How would that benefit you at all?" I ask as I crawl into bed beside Arianna, my heavy eyelids falling closed quickly.

"It would, trust me. So, did you?"

I try to ignore them, but I can feel their gazes on me. Slowly, I peel my eyes open and sigh at them.

"Virginity is firmly intact—sorry to disappoint."

"Booo," Cassi says.

Arianna shakes her head. "Don't listen to her. It's not even her goddamn *business*," she hisses, turning to Cassi.

Cassi rolls her eyes and lies back down. "Whatever. She's our best friend—of course it's our business. Speaking of, I still want that play-by-play of your night in the morning, Ari."

"Whatever you want, Cass," she retorts, laughing as she wiggles down to lie flat.

Thankfully, the room falls quiet and Cassi's snoring is the first sound to fill the room.

Arianna nudges my shoulder with hers.

"Are you okay?" she whispers.

No.

"Yeah, I'm just tired. Crazy night, huh?"

Arianna scoffs and nods. "You're telling me."

***

I wake to Arianna and Cassi whispering about their nights. My sleep-drunk eyes move to the clock, and I see it's already eleven in the morning. It's not hard to sleep in when you don't fall asleep until almost five.

"It was so fucking good, and we swapped numbers. I'm just waiting for him to thirst after me and beg for another night, which I'll gladly give him because my God. Easily the best sex of my life," Cassi says.

Arianna smiles supportively. "So a good birthday then?"

Cassi grins. "A great one. What about you?"

"It was... so fucking good. He's older, like a lot older."

"Ari, did you fuck a GILF?"

Arianna scoffs and shakes her head. "Like forties, Cass."

"I'm just asking," Cassi replies, raising her hands in defense. "Was he the best lay you've ever had?"

Arianna smirks. "He was fucking pierced."

Cassi's scream could make dogs howl—not that she cares.

"Oh my God! I have so many questions. How did it feel for you? For him? Please tell me you burned every moment into your head to relish forever."

Ari laughs. "It was a really fucking good night. I'm not sure how he'll top it next week."

Cassi's smile freezes, the corners drooping ever so slightly. "Next week? He... asked you out?"

Ari shrugs. "Kinda. He asked me to meet him back there. Not sure if that constitutes a date or not."

Cassi stares at her for a moment, like a million thoughts are running through her head. "Well, he might have been saying it in the heat of the moment. You know how men are. I don't want you to get your hopes up."

Ouch. Even I feel the little dig Cassi just threw. Whether she meant to or not, it's out there, and based on Arianna's face, she feels it.

"Did we get late checkout?" I ask, trying to steer the conversation in a new direction.

"Yeah," Arianna says, her tone lacking its former enthusiasm.

"What about you, Nay? Another invite or anything?" Cassi asks.

I shake my head, and she nods like she's relieved, which is

insanely messed up. I mean, she doesn't know that I was left feeling humiliated, embarrassed and... sad.

Still. They should be happy. Cassi got a phone number; Ari got a date. I just got trauma because though I'm trying to block it out, the fact of the matter is I sucked my brother's dick.

After Cassi's moment of... attitude let's call it, we all decided to head out. I live only a few blocks away so it's not bad even with midday traffic. That's the unfortunate thing about Seattle. One o'clock on a Saturday? Traffic. Four in the morning on a Thursday? Traffic. I've never seen a city street empty, and I've lived here my whole life.

As soon as I stroll into the house, I smell something good cooking. Every weekend, we have a family dinner where we can all catch up. Even though Anthony, my oldest brother, lives in Olympia and Nick is constantly traveling for work, they both somehow never miss a dinner. I think they know how much it means to Mom.

"I'm home," I call as I drop my overnight bag by the door.

"In here, sweetheart," my mom says from the kitchen.

I weave my way through our little historic house. It's tight, a three-bedroom, two-bath, 1,100-square-feet home with on-street parking, but it's got a ton of charm to it. It was the home my mom grew up in, and when her parents passed away when she was twenty-two, her and my sperm donor moved in. I say sperm donor because dad just seems like an inappropriate title for a man who fled the state when he found out his wife was pregnant with his third child.

My mom worked her butt off to provide for us kids on her own, especially after she took Kolter in. Granted, Anthony had already moved out by the time Kolter started living with us; still, holidays and weekends were very cramped. I always kinda loved it, though.

"What are we having?" I ask as I step into the kitchen and press a kiss to Mom's cheek.

She smiles and gestures towards the pastry dough she's placing on top of ramekins. "Mini pot pies."

My stomach practically grumbles in celebration and I grin approvingly.

"When will the boys be here?"

She looks down at her phone briefly. "Probably an hour or two—you know Anthony likes to head home early."

I nod. We should honestly start calling it family lunch with how early we do it every week, but hey, who really cares what time of day you eat delicious food, right?

"I'm going to take a quick shower and then I'll help you set the table," I say.

"Sounds good. Wait, did you guys have fun last night?"

I study my mom's warm smile. I don't keep anything from her, so she knows where we went last night. She also knows the status of my sex life—or lack thereof—and that inquisitive smile is very clearly a probe to see if anything monumental happened. As much as I'd love to get this... thing off my chest, I think it would mortify her even more than me, so for once, I keep it all to myself.

"It was... interesting. Still a virgin, to quell your curiosity."

She shrugs. "There's always tomorrow."

I laugh and shake my head before making my way to the upstairs bathroom. Most moms would be pleased that their twenty-one-year-old daughter is still a virgin, right? My mom is less pushy than my friends but more than other mothers I've met. She falls somewhere in the middle of being a compassionate supporter of my choice while also putting pressure on me to use it before I lose it, which I consistently remind her is a ridiculous concept.

After a quick shower, I change into a pair of leggings and a tank top and head downstairs.

The front door opens.

"Mom! We're home," Anthony calls as Nick trails in behind him.

Anthony's eyes meet mine, then he smiles warmly and pulls me in for a hug, pressing a quick kiss to the top of my head. "Hey, munchkin. How was your week?"

"Good. Yours?"

He nods. "Busy, but good."

Anthony has always been more like a dad to me than anything else. A ten-year-age gap and a runaway biological father will do that to you. Neither of us have ever seemed bothered by it, though. He was the one who taught me how to ride a bike; how to change a flat tire. Then there's Nick, who's always been the typical brother.

"High five?" Nick smiles before ripping away his hand and walking past me. "Too slow."

I scoff and shake my head. "Aren't you a little old for that?"

"Nope," he says, popping his P. Then he presses a kiss to Mom's cheek and plops himself down at the dinner table.

"Nicholas, if you don't take your shoes off at the door, I'm going to beat your fucking ass with them," my mom sighs. There's no heat to her words but all the promise in the world.

He snickers at that, quickly kicking off his shoes before jogging over to the front door.

For a twenty-six-year-old, my brother really acts like he's still living that fraternity life.

I help Mom set up everything for dinner, and we fall into easy conversation.

A few minutes later, Nick's phone buzzes with a text. He grabs it and reads it with furrowed brows, then quickly types a message back.

His phone buzzes again.

"Do you have to text at the table?" my mom sighs.

"Sorry, it's just... Kolter texted me."

Tension fills the room as all eyes swing to Nick.

"Kolter?" Mom asks, a soft hopefulness to her tone.

"Yeah, he said he's sorry he hasn't been around in a while and wants to come to dinner next week, if that's okay with you."

"Why didn't he text me himself?" she asks.

Nick shrugs. "You know how he is—probably embarrassed he hasn't been around in years."

Anthony frowns like the news has upset him, and for some reason, his eyes move to me, watching me curiously. I stare back at him for a moment before dropping my gaze to my food.

"Fine, tell him he's always welcome, but don't warn him about the ass-beating I plan to give him for practically disappearing on us these last six years. That boy has a world of hurt coming to him," my mom tsks.

Nick quickly texts him back. Then he smiles. "He says he'll be here next week and he's ready for the wooden spoon."

Mom laughs at that, and Anthony gives a soft nod like he approves, or maybe he just likes that Mom's happy. Me on the other hand? I'm ready to throw up all over this dinner table.

The next day, somewhere in between chores and an extra-credit assignment I'm working on, I find myself lying in bed, staring at the ceiling. My mind is still whirling from what took place in the club.

I reach for my phone and almost word-vomit everything to the group chat before I think better of it. It's not that my friends would ever judge me, but I guess I'm carrying a certain level of shame from that night. Or maybe it's embarrassment? Or maybe I'm just worried that they'll ask if I liked it and I'll have to be honest and tell them yes. So, instead, I opt to stay quiet, at least about my own experience.

I do, however, shoot off a check-in text to Cassi. Arianna is at her family's cabin up north with little-to-no cell reception, and Cassi is dealing with her own brand of torture. Her Mr. Right? The one she was so hooked on from the club? He's her sister's boyfriend. Yep. Boyfriend, as in current. He came with her sister to Seattle to meet the family.

I think it's safe to say he's well acquainted with the family now, so hopefully he's gone.

Me: How did things go today? Is he gone?

Her response comes almost immediately.

Cassi: If by gone, you mean is he staying for an extra week, then absolutely.

My mouth drops open.

Me: WHAT?

Me: EXPLAIN

Me: NOW PLEASE

Obviously, text won't do, but thankfully Cassi is on top of it and sends me a long voice note, which I play immediately.

Gosh, I'm glad I'm not the only one that has their mind spinning.

Chapter Six
Kolter

Her wet pussy bounces up and down on my cock, her moans and whimpers filling the room as her nails dig into my shoulders.

"Fuck! Blade!" she moans, as grating as nails on a goddamn chalkboard.

"Shut your fucking mouth," I hiss as I grip her hips a little tighter and fuck her even harder.

I wouldn't be surprised if she's bleeding by the end of this. That's her thing, though. Out of all the cut sluts who wander around the club, she's the one who likes it to hurt the most. She likes it rough, hard and she doesn't give a fuck what you do to her. As long as she's getting attention, Trinity is in heaven.

Cut sluts are girls with zero morals or self-preservation skills who think they want a taste of this life. They hang with MC gangs and get passed around like a joint at a concert, all because they hope to become someone's ole lady. It happens—sometimes. I don't get it, though; I don't get the idea of settling with anybody in this life. Best-case scenario, you live a few good years before they watch you get gunned down or put away for life. Worst-case scenario, you watch them get gunned down before you follow right behind them. Women are weaknesses, especially in our world. It's better to keep them disposable, like Trinity here.

She does her best to stay quiet like I tell her, but she can't help herself, whining and groaning as her pussy spasms against my cock. I'm nowhere close to done; in fact, I've barely been able to stay hard, which is a first for me. Every time I look at her box-dyed red hair and brown eyes, it sours my stomach.

I lift her off my cock and push her away. She pouts for a moment before dropping to her knees and sucking my cock down her throat. It feels good for a moment, then something else stirs inside me.

Even though I couldn't see her through that glory hole, I knew what she looked like. Sitting at the ready like a good girl, those full, pink lips parted for me; that soft tongue wrapping round me like I was her favorite goddamn treat. I like to think she knew it was me the whole time. Mainly because if I think about her willingly sucking anyone else like that, it makes me want to spill some fucking blood.

Fisting Trinity's hair into my fist, I force her further down my cock, causing her to gag in a way that almost reminds me of Naomi. I do it again and again, relishing in the sound as I close my eyes and let my head rest against the back of the booth.

I didn't know what I was doing when I followed her into the glory-hole hall. Half of me was ready to rip her out by her goddamn hair; the other part was intrigued—what was a naïve little thing like her doing in a place like that? Then some rich prick stepped into the door across from hers. There was no way in hell I was letting him get near her, so I hauled him out of there and threw him to the ground before locking the door. He bitched and whined for help, but the attendant saw me walking in there, and he wasn't about to kick out the club's goddamn owner.

It's easy enough to imagine it's Naomi in front of me, and for the first time tonight, my cock actually throbs. The mouth before me tightens around it, bobbing up and down as my hips mimic her motions.

"Fuck, just like that," I moan.

Eager to please me, she continues quickly, her soft moans of pleasure vibrating along my cock. And just like that, it's not this desperate cut slut before me—it's her. Long blonde hair as smooth as silk, her satin hands gripping my cock, twisting and stroking every drop of cum out of me. It's too good, too perfect, and I don't even try to hold myself back.

"Peaches," I groan through clenched teeth as my load shoots down her throat.

She gags and chokes for a moment, but I force her head into place as I continue to throb my release into her mouth.

When I'm done with her, I shove her away roughly, and she stumbles for a moment before wiping her mouth.

Then a sultry smile crosses her face and she leans into me. "Peaches? Is that my new nickname or something?"

I raise a brow as I pull out a cigarette and light it up. A moment later, I blow smoke in her face. "Now why would I give you a new nickname when Fire Crotch fits you so well," I say, gesturing down to her box-dyed pubes.

She frowns. "I thought you said you liked it."

"I just wanted to see if you would do it, and you did," I scoff.

Her expression turns outraged, but before she can reply, Crow whistles to her from across the room.

"Fire Crotch, bring that pussy over here."

She looks to me like I might save her.

Fat fucking chance.

I turn away, and she skulks begrudgingly over to our oldest and by far heaviest member before climbing into his lap. She knows the deal—she can turn down anyone at any time. No one is gonna force her to do shit. She also knows that if she turns down too many people, she won't be allowed to hang around anymore. Not unless someone lays claim to her.

I look around the semi-empty bar and see not a single other eye is set on her, so that seems unlikely.

Taking another drag of my cigarette, I pull out my phone and read the last text I got from Nick.

Nick: I'm glad you're gonna come by. We all miss you, man.

I don't know what possessed me to reach out to Nick, let alone agree to come to dinner. It's been at least six months since I've seen Nick and years since I've come home for... anything. And there's a good reason for that too.

After everything that went down, I knew what it would mean to keep a close relationship with them. What it would put them at risk for. Back then, I cared too much to do that to them. Now... shit, even I can't convince myself I don't care. They're the best family I ever had. Unlike the piece of shit that's just strolled in here.

My dad struts through the bar like he's a king and this shithole of a bar is his goddamn castle. He looks around his "soldiers" getting drunk or getting some pussy and nods with approval. This lifestyle is unlike anything else, and in his words, the way to keep a man loyal is to keep him content—fill the bar with booze and floozies and they'll never dream of a better place.

I nod at him. "Snakes."

Everyone is given a nickname when they join the club. Some guys still go by their own name, but my dad didn't think Matthew would strike fear into the hearts of his enemies, so Snakes it was. His VP Bones is walking beside him and juts out his chin to me in greeting. They're both in their mid-fifties, and while my dad had me just before my mom passed, Bones never settled down; never had an ole lady or a kid. Their lives are one hundred percent focused around the club now. Being a kid that grew up in and around the club, I gotta say I think it's the way to go.

"Church in ten," my dad says as he walks past me, heading to the back of the house where we host our "church."

No, we don't gather round and talk about the gospel. Church is just what we call our meetings, our time to come together, open our goddamn mouths wide and listen to whatever horseshit he wants to shovel down our throats. Gee, do I sound bitter? It's because I fucking am. I hate him. I hate how he runs this club; I hate how he treats its members. He won't be in charge forever, though. One day, all this will be mine, and I'll be implementing some serious fucking changes.

I push up from the booth and start following them, still puffing on my cigarette.

Bones and my dad are already having a hushed conversation at one end of the table, so I take a seat at the other end, then reach into my pocket and pull out my knife. I flick it open and closed repeatedly, a motion that's become so second nature to me, it's as easy as breathing. Though guns are obviously a cleaner and more effective approach, I've always preferred using them last. Maybe because I know just how goddamn much they hurt.

Chapter Seven
Naomi

I know he told me to stay at the house, but Nick is right. Since Matthew got out of prison, Kolter's been spending all his time with him. He almost never makes it home in time for dinner, he's missed Nick's last three football games, and he didn't even make it to the regionals for my chess team. I know his dad is forcing him to keep his distance; I just can't understand why. We were there for him when he basically abandoned him—we're his real family. He's just a bio-dad. It means nothing. He owes him nothing.

Following him was tricky considering I'm fifteen. No license, no car, which means, yes, I resorted to the hot-pink bike my mom got me for my twelfth birthday. I can barely still fit on it, and it obviously doesn't have a headlight or anything to see at night, but it does the job.

I watch as Kolter pulls into the parking lot of what looks like an abandoned warehouse. We're only a few blocks from the house, but I can honestly say I've never been to this area before. Seattle can turn from urban to sketchy in a matter of a hundred feet or so, and I think it's safe to say we've crossed over into the sketchy district.

I tuck myself behind a tree and watch Kolter greet a man at the door. He's wearing a similar leather vest to Kolter. The only difference is this guy's vest has a patch with a logo instead of the word "prospect."

I looked up what it means to prospect a motorcycle club and hated what I found. Maybe that's why I made the incredibly stupid decision to follow him to what I now understand is some kind of job for the club.

The man that was apparently standing watch outside the warehouse heads for his bike then rides off. Kolter takes up his spot, lighting up a cigarette as he leans against the front door.

I thought he quit years ago. He used to smoke, but when I told him about the dangers of long-term nicotine use, he gave it up like it was nothing. To see that he's still smoking, just behind my back, hurts something inside me, and I can't stop myself from saying something.

"So, you're back to being a smoker?" I call from across the lot.

Kolter's head whips to the side in alarm before his eyes round. I'm stomping my way towards him, but if I thought I'd be the most upset person in this scenario, I was dead wrong. Anger like I've never seen blooms across his face as his heavy boots slam into the pavement towards me.

"Nay? What the fuck are you doing here? Did you follow me?"

I'm frightened by his tone for a moment and swallow roughly as we draw closer. "I just... I wanted to see what you've been doing when you're not at home. Do you just sit out here saturating your lungs with chemicals while you play guard dog?" I say, a little more fire in my tone now.

Finally, we're only a few feet apart so I pause, but that's not close enough for him. He doesn't stop until his steel-toed boots bump into my tennis shoes and his chest hits mine. He looks down at me, those sharp blue eyes I've always loved turning hard and sharp like a knife.

"You need to leave. Now."

"I just don't understand what's happening to you. I used to think I knew you better than anyone. You're my brother," I argue, though the words taste like ash the instant they leave my mouth.

Kolter makes a face as if he doesn't like them either before shaking his head. "I'm serious. This isn't safe—you need to leave before someone sees you."

He grabs my arm and starts to walk me away, but I pull out of his grip and shake my head.

"If it's not safe for me, then it isn't safe for you. I'm not going home until you come with me."

"Goddamnit, Peaches. Do as I fucking say, or I will make you regret it," he threatens, violence flashing in his eyes.

I know I should be scared of him—he's basically threatening me. Deep down, though, I know he'd never hurt me.

I'm about to say as much when a car drives by and a window rolls down. Everything happens so fast. One moment, I'm standing, having it out with Kolter. The next, I'm down on the concrete, his heavy body on top of mine before a loud popping sound echoes through the night.

Looking up, I see Kolter's drawn a gun and is shooting towards the car as it shoots at him. He must hit someone because the car swerves and crashes into a telephone poll. When the passenger door opens, though, two shots are fired simultaneously. One drops the dark-haired man from the car, a perfect hole penetrating his forehead; the other hits Kolter in the chest.

My brain struggles to process what I'm seeing.

Kolter presses his hand to his chest then pulls it away, staring down at the blood coating his fingers.

"Oh fuck," he mutters before dropping to the ground.

Panic races through me as I scramble towards him, frantically scanning his body. Oh God, what do I do? What do I do?

Pressure, right? He needs pressure. And a hospital. Badly.

Quickly, I press one hand against the hole in his chest as I reach for my phone, only to realize I left it on the charger at home. Stupid, stupid!

I pat around in his pockets and find his phone.

"Kolter? Kolter? You're gonna be okay. Okay? Stay with me!"

That's what people on TV say to keep injured people awake, right?

"Peaches," *he rasps.* "Go. You need to go."

"I'm not leaving you!" *I retort as I dial the police.*

"911, what's your emergency?" *the operator asks.*

"Hello! Hi, hello? Help! My friend has been shot."

I look down to see Kolter shaking his head in disapproval, but when he tries to stand, he winces and lies back down fully.

"Okay, what's the address of your location?" *the operator asks.*

"Um, I don't know. Where are we?" *I ask Kolter.*

He reaches up with a shake of his head before grabbing his phone out of my hands. Good, he can probably give an address or something.

Instead of talking to the operator, though, he hangs up the call then tosses the phone to the side.

"No cops," *he rasps.* "They'll kill me, kill you."

"You need help! You've been shot!" *I argue.*

"No, listen!" *he snarls with as much heat as he can muster.* "You need to get out of here—now. Get out of here and don't come back ever. I'll b-be fine. Run!"

"Kolter," *I say, my lower lip wobbling.* "Please let me help."

A tear runs down my face, and he lifts a shaky hand to me, wiping it away with his bloody fingers.

"Help me by keeping yourself safe. Don't tell anyone what you saw, or they'll come for you, you hear me?"

I shake my head. "I can't leave you."

He lets out an aggravated breath as cop sirens sound in the distance. "Help is coming—I'll be fine, Peaches. You won't. Get out of here. NOW!" *he snarls.*

Shakily, I stand, looking down at him as a numbness spreads through me. But I force myself to run for my bike, one foot after the other—though I pause once I'm back in the saddle.

Kolter's eyes are still on me, and even from this distance I can see him nodding to me encouragingly.

Tears are pouring down my face now, but I do as he says and pedal home as fast as I can, praying to God the entire way that he'll live, that God will spare him, that I won't lose him.

I wake up drenched in a cold sweat, my heart beating out of my chest, my breath ragged as I quickly look around my bedroom. It takes my mind a few moments to fully comprehend where I am, that it was all just a dream.

More like a memory.

I haven't dreamed of the last night I saw Kolter in well over a year. It was by far the worst day of my life, and every day that followed for weeks was a new level of hell. Just like I promised him, I didn't tell anyone what I saw. Not even Mom or the boys. I did, however, go looking for him the next morning.

When I got to that old warehouse, the place was empty, the car had been towed and only a few bloodstains remained on the asphalt. I then went to the three closest hospitals to see if he'd been admitted. They all had no record of him, but after looking up the county roster, I finally found him in jail. When I tried to visit, they told me he'd refused to see me. I tried again for three more days, only to be met with the same response each time; then, on the fourth day, I was told that he'd been released.

He wouldn't answer my phone calls, though. Or Nick's, or Anthony's or Mom's. He just... vanished. He didn't check in with any of us until three months later, on Christmas, when he called Mom to tell her he was okay and would be living at the clubhouse from now on. She was upset but told him that he always had a place with us. After all, he was twenty—what could she really do now that he was an adult?

For years, I tried to get in contact with Kolter. Each rejected call felt like a stab to my heart, until finally... I gave up. The pain was so intense I thought I was going to die, and things didn't start to get better until I went to college and forced myself to move... forward, I guess.

Now, I'm prepping the salad for dinner. The dinner that Kolter is supposedly coming to, after six years, out of the blue. Except it's not out of the blue. It can't be a coincidence that after all these years, he finally decides to reach out after I accidentally sucked him off in a sex club.

Was it an accident, though? I mean, it certainly was on my part. But he didn't seem nearly as shocked as I was. In fact, I think he knew it was me the whole time. Why else would he have called out my nickname mid-climax?

That thought is far more intriguing than it should be, and it adds a whole host of nerves to this equation.

The doorbell rings, and I don't know who jumps out of their skin more, me or Nick. Despite the fact he's seen Kolter multiple times over the years, he seems even more excited about this dinner than me.

Nick bounds towards the door and throws it open. "What are you ringing the doorbell like a stranger for? Get in here, brothaaa!"

I hear what sounds like them patting each other's backs as Anthony moves into the hallway, greeting him as well.

"It's been too long, Kol."

"I know. How have you been?" that deep voice rumbles, sending a chill down my spine.

"Really good. You?"

"Just fine. Where's Mom?"

My mom moves from the kitchen and into the dining room, giving Kolter a perfect view of her. She has a wooden spoon in one hand; her other hand is on her hip.

"Oh, now you remember who I am? I was beginning to think you forgot all about me."

I peek round the corner, just enough to see him. He's dressed similarly to the other night—dark clothes, leather cut-off jacket and big boots—his black hair messily styled like the wind's been blowing through it all day.

"Could never forget you," he says as he moves towards her, arms outstretched.

Mom folds easily for him, wrapping her arms around his shoulders and holding him for several seconds. They both whisper to each other, then he lets out a laugh.

Kolter's laugh. It's a sound I almost forgot existed, but when I hear it again, a wave of nostalgia crashes into me. I find myself wanting to search for the nearest jar in the hope I can bottle it up.

"Where did Nay go? Nay! Get in here!" my mom calls out.

Blowing out a slow breath, I square my shoulders and step out of the kitchen. Everyone looks to me, but there's only one set of eyes I can focus on right now. They take me in slowly, moving over me from head to toe as if it's the first time they've ever looked at me.

When his gaze meets mine, anticipation flutters through me, but I do my best to compose myself. I stop a few feet away, mainly because I know if I get any closer, he'll see that I'm literally shaking like a leaf. I don't know why seeing him here is so intimidating to me. I mean, I didn't react nearly this dramatically in the club and I literally sucked him off through a hole cut out of a wall. I was in shock, though, so maybe that had everything to do with it.

Kolter's gaze flicks down to my hands, which I'm discreetly trying to steady. Obviously, I'm not discreet enough because amusement twinkles in his eyes before it's gone altogether.

"Nay, stop being a fucking weirdo and say hi," Nick scoffs.

I roll my eyes at him then turn to Kolter. "Hi."

"Hi," he says in return.

The air is thick between us, so thick I'm certain everyone in this room must be choking on it. Then he does something I don't expect.

He holds out his arms for me. It's a quiet gesture, a simple one, but it speaks volumes to me.

Slowly, I close the distance between us then slip my arms around his waist as his wrap around my shoulders. It feels like he holds me for hours, though it can only be a few seconds.

My heart's beating like a drum in my chest, and when he pulls away, I look up at him, all the questions racing through my head perfectly displayed on my face. Or I hope they are. Can he read them? Does he understand? Sometimes I feel like he used to know my thoughts better than I did, like he could read me better than I could ever articulate. He was... like my other half. I know how corny and weird that sounds, but I don't care. It's true. Or at least, it was.

Instead of giving me even an inkling of a hint one way or another, he offers me a small smile and says, "It's been too long, Peaches."

Peaches.

Just hearing the way his mouth curls around that word has a wave of goosebumps racing across my skin. Then my mom cuts in, telling everyone to take a seat, and I stand there like an idiot for several seconds as Kolter brushes his shoulder against my own.

I turn, watching him and the others take their seats at the table and realize that the only available seat is the one across from him. Not mad about that.

Through dinner, we all lightly catch up as if it was any other dinner. Until it comes time for Kolter to tell us about his week. He pauses, looking around at each of us as if he's trying to come up with a way out of this, then he shrugs.

"Same old stuff. Work, sleep. Hung out with some friends last weekend," he says, his eyes hanging on me when he says *weekend*.

My stomach flips at the reminder, and I try not to get too excited at his casual mention of our... what do you even call that? Hookup? Maybe.

Does that mean he hasn't been able to stop thinking about it all week either? It isn't just me?

After dinner, we all help clean up when Mom gets a phone call and steps away to take it. Nick and Anthony make a start on the dishes already piled up in the kitchen while Kolter and I clear the others from the table. We work in silence, though I keep checking to see if he's watching me, but to my disappointment, his eyes stay busy on his task. Nerves bounce around inside me—then I truly don't know what takes over me.

Glancing up to make sure we're out of sight of Nick and Anthony as they laugh and chat in the kitchen, I clear my throat, earning Kolter's gaze.

"We need to talk," I say.

Kolter lifts a brow in question but doesn't respond.

Swallowing roughly, I set the cups in my hand back on the table then walk round to him, still checking to make sure we're out of sight. I stop a few inches away. He keeps the plates in his hands as he draws himself up to his full height, looking down at me with a blank face as I blow out a heavy breath.

Okay, Nay. Here we go. All our cards on the table.

"Last weekend. It was... unexpected. I mean, I haven't seen you in years, then to see you like that... I was shocked and caught off guard. I hardly had a moment to process what was going on, who it was going on with. I mean, it was sensory overload in there, an over-stimulation nightmare really, and I—"

"Peaches," he cuts off my speed-rambling tersely before giving me a look. "Your point?"

I take a breath then continue, much slower this time. "My point is... What would you say if I told you that I liked it? Last weekend. What would happen if I told you I wanted it to happen again?"

Something like surprise flashes in his eyes for a moment before a soft smile curves his face. Slowly, he lowers himself to me so our faces are only inches apart, his next words whispered against my lips.

"What would you say if I told you I'd forgot all about it?"

Shock reverberates through me at his words; at the cold, callous tone that matches his impassive expression.

He pulls away, straightening once more, then turns and heads for the kitchen with the plates.

It's as if I can feel my heart cracking in my chest, so I have no choice but to run upstairs and hide in humiliation.

Chapter Eight
Kolter

"Where's the shipment coming in to?" I ask before my fist lands, snapping the guy's head to the side.

My knuckles burn—a few of them have split open from the impact of my blows. I'm doing a hell of a lot better than this guy, though. Blood covers nearly every inch of his face, his head lolling on his shoulders like a wet mop as he babbles incoherently.

I grab hold of his sweat-and-blood-soaked hair and yank his head backward so he's forced to look at me. "Tell me where the fucking shipment is coming in and you'll be home by dinner," I snarl.

The guy is a low-level soldier of the Volkov family, the Russian bratva around this area, and our number one pain in the fucking ass. They steal our shit; we take theirs. They claim territory; we gut them like pigs and take what's owed to us. There are a few other motorcycle clubs around the Seattle area, but we've been here the longest. This is our city, and no one, especially not some little Russian punk, is gonna get in the way of that. So, yet again, I'm asking where the fuck their coke shipment is landing. They've intercepted our last two shipments, so an eye for an eye and all that shit.

"If I don't tell you, I won't go home," he wheezes in a thick Russian accent. "And if I tell, I won't go home."

A smile curves my mouth as I pull his head back even further, making sure he's able to see every glimmer of violence coming his way. Seems to work too—the guy blanches beneath the blood covering his face before swallowing roughly.

"You're a smart kid."

His breathing is ragged, but I can hear a definite wheeze. Could be a collapsed lung. Apparently, he fought pretty hard when we scooped him off the street. I wasn't part of that, though—I'm just here to handle the questioning.

Ace and Brick are leaning against the warehouse wall, bullshitting and smoking cigarettes while I do all the heavy lifting. But I can tell this kid isn't ready to talk yet, so he can be their fucking problem until he softens up.

I step away from him and move over to my bag of goodies, rifling through until I pull out two nine-inch knives. I admire them as they glint in the setting sunlight then look back at the bratva brat.

"You sure you're not up for a chat?" I ask.

He watches me hesitantly but stays silent.

I admire that. It's the only way to stay alive in this world. You don't narc, ever. You get kidnapped by the enemy, you're basically already dead. And if you do escape and they find out you narced, you're gonna wish the enemy had killed you.

I shrug then bury the knives into his thighs. He lets out an ear-piercing shriek that reverberates through the warehouse. Thank fuck we're in the middle of fucking nowhere right now.

He howls and whimpers, fighting against his restraints as I watch. I shake my head. If he'd stop moving, it wouldn't hurt so much. Fucking pussy.

Okay, maybe that's a lie. I sank those fuckers all the way through. Still.

I turn away from the whimpering mess in the chair and head for the door.

Brick nods to me as Ace gestures towards the guy. "What do you want us to do with him?"

"Take turns watching him. He needs some time to think on how loyal he wants to be to his 'family.' I'll be back in the morning."

Ace nods then turns to Brick. "I'll catch second shift," he says before heading out the door with me.

"Aw man, what the fuck? You know my ole lady's got dinner cooking. She's gonna have my nuts."

Ace shrugs like he couldn't care less. "Told you not to settle down, man. You brought this on yourself."

Brick curses under his breath before whipping out his phone, no doubt to let his girl know he won't be home as planned. That's just the reality of our work, though. He gets it, and so does she. There aren't a lot of women connected to the Black Crows for this very reason. We aren't a leisure club; we don't hustle a little weed or guns once in a while. This is an empire, an economy. Once you're in it, you're in it, and the only way out is in a wooden fucking box.

My dad made all of that very clear to me when he got out of prison all those years ago. I'd resisted prospecting the club, leaning towards the same all-American dream Nick was chasing. That we both were. But Snakes made it very clear that not only would that be a poor decision; it would be an impossible one, on his orders.

"You heading back to the club?" Ace asks.

I shake my head as I throw my leg over my bike and fire it up.

He frowns, cocking his head to one side. "You good, man? You've been extra... edgy lately."

I want to scoff at him. No, I'm not fucking good. Not since I walked into that goddamn club, that goddamn room and shoved my cock through that hole. Not since she began plaguing every thought of every moment of my life afterwards. She's like an infection, and I want her gone. The only thing I can think to do is starve her out of my system, but with every growing day, the pain of doing that is becoming damn near unmanageable.

I'd never admit any of that shit to another living soul, though. So, instead, I shrug and reach my hand out to his. He bumps his fist against mine warily before nodding his acceptance and firing up his own bike.

Ace prospected the club a little after I joined up, so we've known each other for a while, and I'm sure he'd consider us great friends. He's an alright guy—good in a fight, takes orders well—but that's about as close as I'll ever get to someone in the club. Honestly, to anyone anywhere.

When I pull up to a stop light, I feel my phone buzz in my jacket, and I quickly pull it out.

Nick: Hey, man. Game's on tonight. Want to meet up?

He stopped asking me years ago. I guess now I've been to dinner, he assumes the door is open. Fuck, I wish I could leave it open. I've missed Nick. He wasn't just a friend; he was my goddamn brother. Seeing him, even Anthony and Mom... it was like the hole in my chest was temporarily patched. The only thing that brought the good vibes down was sitting at the table with *her*.

Before I've thought it through, I'm responding to him, shooting off a text just before the light turns green.

Me: Sure. Meet me at the GOAT.

It's a sports bar that's almost considered Northgate—out of the direct jurisdiction of the Black Crows and hopefully far enough away from anyone that could spot us. The last thing I want is Nick getting caught up in any of this shit.

Nick must have been in the area because he beats me to the bar. As soon as I walk in, a goofy-ass grin lights up his face, then he's jumping off the bar stool and making his way over to me. He pulls me in for a quick hug, clapping my back as he nods to his seat.

"C'mon—I got the first round ordered."

I sit down and take the beer Nick offers me, dipping my head in thanks.

"I wasn't sure you were gonna accept the invite," Nick says, almost hesitantly.

"I wasn't sure I was gonna either," I reply then take a sip of my beer.

"I've missed you, bro. I'm glad you're around."

I don't know how to tell him that I won't be around for much longer. I can't be. The more times I hang with him, go to Mom's, anything, the higher the chance of someone catching on. And then no one is safe. I'm not bringing my life into theirs; I'll die before I let that happen. Instead of saying all that, though, I nod and shrug like it's no big deal.

"I've missed you too," I say before turning my attention to the TV in front of us.

Nick does the same, and as time goes by and drinks go down, we both loosen up—until we're screaming and hollering when our boys pull a home run out of their asses.

"Fuck yeahhhh!" Nick shouts before high-fiving a stranger and then me.

I laugh at his tipsy ass as he wobbles on the stool, and he grins back at me.

"Fuck, man. Why haven't we been doing this all this time? It's bullshit."

I nod. "I'm sorry."

Nick shrugs, pushing my shoulder and waving me off. "S'no big deal. Anthony was never upset, and you've won Mom's forgiveness."

He's left someone out, and I can't tell if it's on purpose or not. Despite knowing better, I can't help but ask.

"And Naomi?"

Nick moves his gaze from the TV to me then back to the TV. "What about her?"

"Does she forgive me? Or was she ever upset that I kinda... ghosted."

Nick laughs then shakes his head. "You're kidding, right? Nay was a fucking mess when you went off with your dad. She used to cry every fucking night. Stopped eating dinner at the table because she'd just sit there and stare at your empty seat. Mom was ready to put her in goddamn therapy. It tore her up, man."

Shock slams into me. Maybe I assumed she'd be upset, or even a darker part of me hoped it. I didn't know it was... like that, though.

"You never told me," I say quietly.

Nick and I had loosely stayed in touch, but he'd only ever tell me the family was good. Small updates about him or Anthony, sometimes even Naomi. But never once did he mention she was... struggling.

Nick's light-hearted smile dims, and he shrugs. "I didn't want you to feel bad. I know you did what you had to do. In a way, Mom did too. Nay, though? She was too young. She didn't get it."

"She's not that much younger than us," I point out quickly.

"Maybe not in years, but she's sheltered. I don't even think she knows what an MC does. Hell, I'm sure I don't have a clue," he says, laughing, then gestures to my split-open hands, which are resting on the bar.

Slowly, I move them into my lap out of view as Nick claps my shoulder.

"Don't sweat it, man. She's grown up a lot. College has been good for her. She's dated a few guys. Still has her two best friends by her side. If she's still holding a grudge, I'm sure she'll let it go soon."

"Who?" I ask sharply.

"Hm?"

"Who has she dated?"

Nick looks to the ceiling like he's trying to remember the names.

"Uh, there was one dude she went to prom with—Ben or Brad or some shit. He was a tool. Then there was... oh fuck, what was his name? I think Marc? He was a few years younger than me but in my fraternity."

An irrational level of anger pulses through me just imagining any of those little weasel fucks putting their hands on her, taking her out, touching her.

My fists curl tightly in my lap, and I close my eyes as I do everything I can to reign in my anger. I have no right to feel this way. I wasn't around. I'm sure they were good guys, and Naomi has always been a smart girl. It still doesn't kill my desire to hunt every one of those motherfuckers down and make sure they treated her right; make sure they didn't place one goddamn toe out of line.

Nick clearly doesn't get it—he couldn't because I never let him in on any of this shit. Leaving was one of the hardest things I ever had to do, but it wasn't about school or him or even Mom. It was leaving her that nearly killed me. And apparently, it nearly killed her too.

Chapter Nine
Naomi

I'm lying in bed, replaying dinner from the other night over and over in my head. Each time I do, it cracks my chest open a little more, like my own personal brand of torture. I have to stop. I have to push him and that night at the club out of my head once and for all. It was a mistake, clearly, and the only way forward is pretending it never happened.

Even I don't buy my own crap, though.

Spring break is almost over, and I'm not going to waste it wallowing over Kolter. I've done enough of that to last me a lifetime.

I make my way downstairs and find Mom sitting at the table, enjoying breakfast before her shift starts. She works so hard, even to this day. I know she doesn't have a clue how amazing she is. Once I'm finished with college, I'm going to get an amazingly good job and help her get ahead of... everything. She deserves to take a break, slow down, live.

"Morning, sweet girl," my mom says, smiling as I press a kiss to the top of her head.

"Morning, Mama," I reply, taking a seat beside her.

"Any fun plans for the day? Spring break is almost over," she reminds me.

Honestly, don't need the reminder. I enjoy school, and I'm kinda bored without it. I contemplated getting a part-time job like Cassi, but with all the advanced classes I take, my workload is full. Still, a job would help during breaks like this.

I shrug. "Not really."

My mom nods then rises from the table and heads over to the sink to rinse out her cereal bowl. Yes, my mom is nearly fifty and still eats cereal almost every morning. She says she'll never stop, and we all think it's hilarious.

"God," she sighs. "I just... I can't believe Kolter came over the other day. I was beginning to wonder if we'd ever see him again."

My stomach instantly turns at the mention of him, and I find myself searching for the nearest exit. Mom turns to face me when I don't respond then tilts her head to one side.

"Is everything okay? I know you took his leaving harder than all of us. That's why I thought you'd be happy to see him."

"I was—I mean, I am. It was fine." I pause, cursing my awkward rambling. "He's just... not the guy he used to be, you know?"

My mom's smile turns sad. "No doubt because of his good-for-nothing father. I swear to God, if I ever cross paths with that man again, I'll run him over with my car."

My eyebrows shoot up in surprise at the intensity of her words. My mom is a kind woman, a gentle one; I rarely see her get fired up. But there are two topics she never discusses—Kolter leaving and our father. Now that one of those topics has been brought up, it's easy to see why she tends to avoid it altogether.

"Well, let's hope you never cross paths with him. That's murder, and you wouldn't do well in prison."

My mom snorts. "You're right about that."

I smile sadly as she sighs.

"I just... I wish I could turn back time. As soon as I got custody of

Kolter, I would have taken all of you kids and ran—gone somewhere he'd never find us. Then he could never have sunk his claws into Kolter. I imagine how different his life could be if I'd been a little braver."

I frown. "Mom, you can't blame yourself. Besides, it's not like Kolter seems to have a bad life."

She shakes her head. "You don't know what their world is like. How dangerous it is. The horrors those men have to go through for the sake of Matthew's whims."

"And you do?" I challenge.

She hesitates for a moment before nodding. "You have to remember—I grew up with him. His dad was at least twice as terrible as he was. Matthew was always a mean-spirited person, but the MC, his dad, it all amplified it. Kolter, though," she says with a heavy exhale. "He was good; he still is. I just worry about how that world is treating him. I worry he'll grow into a man I'm not familiar with, and that will break my damn heart."

I sometimes forget how deeply seeded Kolter is in our family. Too blinded by my own selfish desires, I forget that my mom effectively lost a son; that my brothers lost a sibling. I thought I'd suffered the worst of it, but, in reality, I'm only one of the many casualties.

"I'm glad he's come back around," I say carefully. "I'm glad you have him back."

My mom looks to me with a soft smile. "Not sure how long it will last, but I'll drink in the moments with all you kids while I can."

I dreamed about him last night, though it's every night these days. I swear, the more I try to push him out of my head, the more he infiltrates my every waking thought. I'm getting so fucking sick and tired of it. I just need... a break. I tried to call Arianna, but she didn't answer, so I FaceTime Cassi instead.

It takes a few rings before the screen comes to life, then Cassi smiles and waves as she props up the phone and begins making what looks like nachos.

"Hey, what's up?" she asks.

"Nothing, just needed a distraction. What are you up to?" I ask as I lie back on my bed.

"Making a snack. You?"

"Starving. What are you making? I can be over in five," I say, laughing, though I'm a hundred percent serious.

Cassi tenses for a moment before laughing me off. "No way, moocher."

My laughter softens as my brows pull together. "Wait, where are you? That doesn't look like your kitchen. Oh my God. Are you at Alec's house?"

She did tell me that she's been seeing her ex-boyfriend recently. I love that for her. He adored her, practically worshipped the ground she walked on, and we all thought they were going to be endgame. He's handsome, sweet and, most importantly, not a cheating piece of shit like her sister's boyfriend.

Cassi grabs the phone, quickly abandoning the nachos, and steps outside, laughing nervously. "Um, nooo."

I tilt my head to the side, waiting for her to explain where she is. Instead of saying anything, though, she just stares at me with a guilty look.

"Cass, where are you?" I ask calmly.

"I'm, uh, in Boston."

"Boston? Since when?"

Classes start on Monday. What could she be doing there? I mean, I know her sister lives out there, but she just visited Seattle and they've never been close, so it's not like she followed her out there for more family bonding or anything like that.

"I got here yesterday," Cassi says quietly.

Wait. No. Oh my God.

I can't help it. My mouth drops open, and my eyes widen as I look at my best friend, who's making a huge fucking mistake.

"Cass... no."

Tucking a piece of hair behind her ear, Cassi looks down at the ground nervously. "Yeah, I mean, it just kinda happened."

"What do you mean?" I gasp. "What just happened? You sleeping with your sister's boyfriend, or you jumping on a plane so you have easier access to him?"

Cassi seems shocked by my aggression, but come on—we've always been straight with each other. Especially Cassi, honestly. She's the first one to tell us when someone's doing something fucked up. Just because she's the one in that position now doesn't mean she gets a free pass.

"I..."

"Honestly, I'm really disappointed in you, Cass. I mean, this isn't you. I know you and Carly don't get along, but to help her boyfriend cheat? The club was an accident, but this," I say as I gesture to the men's button-down she's currently wearing.

Cassi quickly pinches the shirt together, like that will absolve her of what she's done. Don't get me wrong, I'm not trying to judge her. She's a grown woman—she can sleep with whoever she wants, and as her friend, it's my job to support whatever makes her happy. This isn't that, though. She felt awful when she found out her mystery man was her sister's boyfriend. We talked for hours about how she regrets it and wants him to disappear—a feeling I can absolutely relate to. That's why I'm so dang confused why she's doing this.

"You don't get it," Cassi says with a shake of her head, her voice choked with tears.

"No, I don't. At all. This isn't you. You're worth more. You're not a side piece; you don't deserve your sister's sloppy seconds. You deserve someone like Alec that will make you their entire life. You should be number one, always."

I hope she understands where I'm coming from because it's true. She deserves the world. Not this slimy scumbag.

"Would you believe me if I told you that Nico makes me feel that way?" Cassi asks quietly.

"Not if he's still dating your sister," I answer honestly.

Hurt flashes on her face, and for a moment, I regret being so hard on her.

"It's complicated, Nay," she snaps defensively.

Complicated? *Complicated?* Call me the dang queen of complicated. At least she didn't suck off her brother. At least she isn't dreaming of doing it again and again. The difference is, I'm refusing to go there. I know it's wrong, and so does he. I mean, yes, I did try to initiate another encounter, but that was a lapse of judgment, and I needed the brush-off from Kolter to fully take in the situation. It's wrong, it's messed up, and I know better. Cassi should too. Instead, she's playing the victim, and it pisses me off.

"It's more than complicated, Cass. It's wrong."

The hurt dissipates from her features then, fiery rage taking over.

"I get that you don't have all of the facts and you're drawing conclusions based off the information you have, but respectfully, you don't know what the fuck you're talking about."

I laugh bitterly as she continues to defend herself with absolutely zero self-reflection. "Okay, Cass. Play the victim. I'm the bad guy, Carly is the bad guy. Not you and Nico, though, right? You guys are just two innocents caught up? Like it's that fucking easy. Society has rules, standards, and you're breaking them!"

I'm practically heaving. I never swear—my mom instilled that in me from a young age, so I've probably cursed a total of five times my whole life. Six now, I guess.

Cassi shakes her head in disbelief and sneers at me. "Honestly, why am I getting lectured by a jealous virgin? Maybe if you stuffed more than vibrators in your cunt, you'd chill the fuck out and realize life isn't so black and white! It's messy, and I thought my best friend would get that. Apparently not. Do the world a favor and get laid already—you're acting like a miserable bitch."

The screen goes dark, and I'm left feeling numb. That's the problem with fighting with friends—they know just how to hurt you.

Without thinking about it, I stand up and move to my closet, rifling through my clothes until I find the shortest, tightest dress possible. It's a little black dress that's even more risqué than the one I wore to the club. Ari got it for me for my birthday last year, knowing I'd never buy it for myself.

A small part of me is afraid Cassi is right. Maybe I am so uptight, so miserable all the time because I keep myself locked away. Well, tonight, things will be different. Fuck it.

Chapter Ten
Naomi

My heels are high, my lips are painted red, and my legs are shaved and oiled to the point they practically slip against each other as I walk the streets of Seattle. In hindsight, maybe I should have found someone to come with me—Capitol Hill isn't exactly the safest area. Then again, even on a weeknight, there are tons of people going in and out of bars and nightclubs. I'm sure I'll be fine.

I haven't gone out much, at least not by myself, so I don't know where the best places are. Part of me even contemplated going back to the sex club, but I quickly put that thought out of my head. Tonight is about empowerment. If I meet someone and they're hot and we end up sleeping together... well, I'm not saying no. I'm also not going out in search of it either.

Finally, I stop at a club that has some familiar dance music playing. There—decision made. If the place sucks, at least the music won't.

I walk over to join the line, but a moment later, the doorman waves me over to him. Frowning, I slowly step out of the queue and obey. I don't know why I'm nervous—it's not like I've done anything wrong. I got in the correct line, right? Is he going to tell me I'm not dressed appropriately, or maybe they're at capacity and I shouldn't bother waiting. I really wish every moment of my life didn't send me into a spiraling meltdown, but here we are.

When I reach the man, I begin twirling the handle of my purse nervously. "Is everything okay?" I ask.

He nods. "ID?"

I hesitate for a moment before pulling out my driver's license. He looks at it quickly then steps to the side.

"Come on in."

I look back at the long line of people who are now glaring at me. I've never been that person who cuts lines or even thinks they're good-looking enough to do so. How embarrassing would that be if you got called out for it and sent to the back of the line? Nope, no way. Couldn't be me. I'd crawl into the dumpster round the corner before I did that.

I look back at the bouncer, who still has his arm extended, his patience clearly waning, then decide to step through.

Instantly, I'm immersed in a dark hallway which then breaks through to a room filled with bright flashing lights. There's a live band on stage and people dancing everywhere.

This is why it's helpful to go out with friends—you never feel awkward or out of place with them. But when you're by yourself, everyone's eyes come to you, almost like you have the word "loser" stamped across your forehead. Okay, that's probably just my insecurity coming out, but that's how it feels as I carefully move through the crowd towards the bar.

"What can I get ya?" the bartender shouts over the beat.

"Um, vodka tonic?"

He nods, grabs a bottle of vodka from behind him and quickly mixes the drink.

"Want to keep it open?" he asks as I hand him my card.

I look around the place. Despite feeling a little uneasy that I'm alone, I'm starting to get used to it.

"Yes please."

He nods, swipes it then hands it back to me, along with my drink.

I take a sip and wince as the alcohol singes the back of my throat. No pain, no gain, right? Technically, I think that saying is about working out, but I think mustering as much liquid courage as possible should count too.

I throw the rest of the drink back, cringing again at the burn, then catch the bartender's attention as I set my glass on the bar.

"Another please."

He nods and pours me another as someone drops a card on the counter beside me. A man with a bright white smile, blue eyes and dirty blonde hair smiles down at me before talking to the bartender.

"Put it on my tab, Nicky. I'll do a double shot of Pendleton."

"You got it," the bartender says to the guy, who's already back to smiling at me.

"I'm Brett," he says, holding out his hand for me to shake.

I look down at it for a moment, and I can feel myself shrinking back. Why, though? He's handsome, showing interest in me and seems nice so far. Isn't this the exact reason I came out tonight? To get out there, get some experience? In this case, that means not running away the instant a good-looking guy looks my way.

"Naomi," I say with a small smile, forcing my anxiety to the side as I shake his hand.

He grins. "Beautiful."

The bartender returns with our drinks, and Brett lifts his to me with a smile.

"Cheers."

I clink my glass against his then knock the drink back in one chug. I cough through the sting of the alcohol, and Brett looks at me curiously before nodding to the dance floor.

"You want to dance?"

"Um... sure. Let's."

I only hesitated for a second there. Look at me go.

Brett shoots his drink in one go too, then offers me his hand and guides us through the crowded dance floor. Bodies brush into us occasionally, but when I look at them, I see that everyone is just too lost in their own moment to care, and I kinda love that.

When we're in the center of the crowd, Brett turns to face me, sliding one arm around my lower waist as he begins swaying to the music. I dance in place for a moment before deciding to be a little braver. I inch towards him a little at a time, but when he notices this, he grins and yanks me against him, forcing his leg in between my thighs. I gasp at the brazen move, and he ducks his head down to whisper against my ear.

"You're so fucking hot."

I smile up at him from beneath my lashes then rest my hands on his biceps, and steadily, we find a rhythm, dancing to song after song. The alcohol is pulsing through me already, especially with the empty stomach I'm currently working with. That's why when Brett gets us another round and I slam it just like the others, the whole world starts to spin. Or maybe that's the dancing. I couldn't really tell you.

The tempo picks up as the song shifts, and Brett's hands begin to wander. Panic starts to rise inside me, but I force it away. This is exactly the kind of stuff Cassi was talking about. I play things too safe; I don't take risks. I run before anything exciting can ever happen in my life.

But not tonight.

Brett slips a hand beneath my dress, slowly snaking his way towards my panties as he smiles down at me and presses his lips to mine. The kiss catches me by surprise, and that nervous ball in my stomach intensifies. But in a good way I think? Honestly, the drinks have me all but floating, and I'm not sure I could stop if I wanted to right now. I don't want to, though—I think.

I kiss him back and start to wind my arms around his neck, mainly for stability—and then I'm suddenly ripped backward. I stumble several feet before landing on my ass, the thud audible even over the loud beat of the song, and several people stare at me while a man in a leather jacket has Brett's shirt balled in his fists. They shout at each other for a moment, but I can't really make out what they're saying. Then the leather-jacket dude rears his head back before cracking Brett in the nose.

Brett stumbles backward, and several people rush to check on him. One man even tries to pull the guy in the leather jacket away, but that Good Samaritan is rewarded with a sucker punch to the face before Brett's attacker turns to me. The instant he does, my heart sinks.

I don't know if it's the alcohol or if I really am seeing what I'm seeing right now, but that's Kolter stalking towards me, undiluted rage on his face. He bends down then throws me over his shoulder, and the entire world tips upside down. A wave of nausea slams into me. I gag for a moment as we step out of the bar, and Kolter growls at me over his shoulder.

"You better not fucking puke on me."

Well, he's asked so nicely, I'm semi-tempted.

"Where're we going?" I slur.

Dang, I guess I'm more buzzed than I thought.

I feel him shake his head. "To get you sober," he grumbles.

"I'm fine!" I argue. "I wanna dance. Let me go!" I shout and begin beating on his back.

My blows don't affect him in the slightest, though his arms do tighten around my legs, like he's expecting me to start kicking. Not a bad plan.

"Yeah, I don't think your dance partner is up for another song," he sneers.

"What about you?" I ask. Realizing quickly how that sounds, I add, "I mean, if he's hurt, so are you, right? A headbutt isn't a good idea for anyone."

In an instant, my world is flipped on its head once more, Kolter swinging me forward until I land on my feet. My ankles buckle, thanks to my heels, so he holds me under the arms, keeping me from sprawling on the sidewalk as he stares down at me.

"I've got a hard head."

I can't help but laugh at that and nod in agreement. "You don't have to convince me you're hard-headed."

His eyes narrow like daggers before he grabs the front door to a diner. "How can you be this buzzed and still a smart-ass?" he asks, gesturing for me to step inside.

"How can you be this grumpy and still so cute?" I wonder, a giggle escaping before I can stop myself.

Oh my gosh. Did I just say that out loud?

Kolter is staring at me with a blank expression, so I rush into the diner, hoping to avoid eye contact with him—for the rest of my life if possible.

I grab a seat in a booth then cradle my head in my hands. The world hasn't stopped spinning since Kolter first tipped me upside down, and sadly I don't see any relief in sight.

I listen to his heavy footsteps as he approaches, but he doesn't sit down. Slowly, I lift my head out of my hands and look up at him.

"You're in my seat," he says flatly.

My brows furrow as I look to the other side of the booth. "They're identical."

His expression is hard and unyielding as he continues to stare me down. "This one faces the door. I always face the door."

Sighing, I stand up, wobbling for a moment, then switch to the other seat. "What? You think danger is going to come bursting in through a diner door?"

"Yes," Kolter says as he finally sits, assessing his surroundings like he's a security guard or something.

I shake my head then rest it in my hands once more. "You're paranoid."

"And you're naïve, Peaches."

"Don't call me that," I grumble.

"Why?"

I lift my head then rest it against my arm so I'm looking up at him. "Because it reminds me of a time where you liked me, and then I get sad because we don't live in that time anymore."

His brows knit together, but the waitress comes over before he has a chance to say anything. Not like he would have, though.

"What can I get you two?" she asks dryly.

"Two black coffees, and the greasiest burger you have for her. Lots of fries and ranch."

She nods and jots the order down on her pad before walking away, while I just stare at the confusing man in front of me. He's not looking at me, though. Instead, it's like he's casing the place. His gaze continues swinging around, looking through the windows down the street, up the road then back to the door. As if anyone would want to bother with us. Then again, what do I know? He's the one with this mysterious life in a dangerous motorcycle gang. Maybe he has enemies out there right now hunting him down. Far-fetched, but you never know.

The coffees come then, and we both drink them easily. Though I usually prefer cream and sugar with mine, it definitely helps sober me up—as does the enormous burger I'm given ten minutes later.

We sit there in total silence, but once I've gathered enough composure, I find the courage to ask a question that's been thrumming in my head since I first saw him.

"How did you know where I was?"

He looks away from the window to me, his gaze flicking across my face for a moment. "I didn't."

I don't believe him for a second, but he clearly won't tell me the truth, so I switch tactics.

"Okay, well, why did you interrupt us?"

"Excuse me?" he asks, raising one eyebrow.

"Me and Brett—that's the name of the guy you headbutted in case you were curious."

"I wasn't."

I shake my head in disbelief. What happened to the sweet boy I grew up with? The one that smiled more than he frowned. The one I could talk to for hours and never get bored of. This version is cold, stoic, and downright miserable to be around.

"Why did you insert yourself into the situation? We were having a great time. Everything was consensual, and—"

"Was it? Did you seriously not see the little baggie in his shirt pocket? The one he was about to roofie you with? Come the fuck on, Peaches. I know you're naïve, but even you know better than to go out clubbing by yourself, and you don't even open your goddamn eyes? That piece of shit would have ripped through your virginity so fast then left you bleeding in the goddamn alley without even thinking twice," Kolter snarls.

My eyes round as my stomach sours.

What?

I sit there for a moment, trying to process everything he's just told me. He could be making it up to scare me? Based on the look on his face, though, I'd guess he's dead serious. Which is absolutely terrifying.

"I didn't know," I whisper to myself.

Kolter leans back into his seat, nodding as he looks out the window. "You can say thank you now."

The words don't come easy. In fact, they don't come at all. We end up sitting in silence once more until I've had my fill of food, then Kolter drops a large bill on the table and stands up. I follow behind him as he pushes open the door, and we make our way onto the sidewalk.

I'm walking almost on the curb, trying to keep some distance between us as I continue to process the night's events—and what could have happened. Then Kolter curses under his breath and grabs my elbow, yanking me to the side so that I'm on the inside of the street and he's now walking on the curb.

"Jesus Christ, Nay. It's not fucking rocket science. The man walks closest to the road; he maintains a visual of all possible exits. Have your brothers taught you nothing?"

"Guess you haven't," I throw back coldly.

His expression tenses for a moment before he shakes his head, pulling out a cigarette and lighting it. He takes a few irritated drags of it then continues down the road, only stopping when he reaches a bike.

It's not like the one he used to ride. It looks newer, bigger.

He grabs a helmet from the back of the bike and hands it to me. Then he swings his leg over the bike and fires it up—but I'm still just standing there holding the helmet.

"Are you coming or what?" he snarks.

"Where?"

He sighs. "Home. I'm taking you home before anything else can fucking happen to you."

I frown and cross my arms. "Why would you care?"

He looks at me like I'm being difficult on purpose then shouts, "Goddamnit, Peaches, will you just get on the fucking bike?"

Slowly, I move towards him, trying unsuccessfully to put the helmet on. He scoffs and yanks me closer, fastening it for me, his face only inches from mine.

"I thought you never wanted me on a bike," I whisper.

I'm so quiet, he shouldn't be able to hear me over the roaring sound of his exhaust. He does, though, and those intense eyes snap to mine.

"That was when you were a kid. Looks like you're all woman now."

I look down at my skimpy dress and instantly feel naked, but

Kolter turns his head away so he's facing forward as he gestures for me to hop on. Carefully, I swing my leg over and sit there for a moment, unsure what to do with my hands.

He unleashes another aggravated sigh before tossing his cigarette on the ground, grinding it out with his foot then grabbing my hands in his. He forces me to grip his torso as he flicks the kickstand up and rolls us backward into the road.

"Hold on tight and keep your dress tucked in. I don't want to have to beat the piss out of some fucker who accidentally sees all of you."

I have a hard time understanding why that would matter to him, but then he takes off down the road, and the thought goes flying out of my head. For a moment, I feel like we're going to tip over, mainly due to my imbalance, so I plaster myself against his back and hold on to him as tightly as possible, to the point that my arms are shaking from the strain. Kolter grunts, no doubt because I'm strangling his stomach. He doesn't ask me to stop, though.

We sail through the streets, weaving in and out of traffic as if we're floating instead of driving. Slowly, my fear starts to ebb as I realize how good a driver Kolter is. Still, my heart races when we take a sharp corner that almost has us meeting the pavement, and I let out a yell. It's a mix of excitement and fear, and when Kolter pulls the bike upright, I'm full-on giggling. I can't help it.

I continue laughing the entire way home, and I even catch the smallest hint of a smile on Kolter's face when he checks in on me. It makes me laugh harder, and I can't help but feel a sense of disappointment when he pulls into our driveway and turns off the bike.

He flicks the kickstand into place before sliding off the bike. I'd do the same, but honestly my legs are shaking from a combination of the adrenaline and the bike's vibrations. It's enough that I bet you could get off from the vibrations alone, if you were properly motivated.

Kolter reaches out, undoing the helmet then hooking it onto one of the handlebars. My smile still hasn't left my face, and he looks down at me with something that isn't quite a smile, but isn't a frown either.

"You have fun?"

I nod. "I can't believe you never let me ride before. That was... amazing."

He offers his hand to help me get off the bike, and I swing my leg over it carefully so I'm not flashing my... everything.

A heavy silence falls between us.

I glance at the house then back to him. "Thank you."

Kolter stares at me quietly, as if he wants me to be more specific. I try to suppress my eyeroll because he can be so freaking obnoxious.

"For taking me home, for sobering me up and... for helping me."

He nods—and then the lecture begins. "I'm not always going to be around, Peaches. You have to take better care of yourself."

I shrug. "I never do stuff like this."

"Then why did you tonight?" he pushes.

I freeze for a moment, looking down at my feet awkwardly before shrugging again.

A finger slips under my chin, forcing my eyes up to meet his. His expression is still hard, but there's a softness in his gaze. He doesn't ask again, mainly because I know he expects me to answer him the first time.

I chew on the inside of my lip and let out a soft sigh. "I just wanted to get out there, prove that I could meet people, cut loose. I don't know."

"You now see why that wasn't a smart choice," he replies.

Embarrassment hits me, and I duck my head. But that finger pulls my chin right back up, his face a few inches closer this time. My gaze flicks back and forth between his eyes and his lips. So full and soft—a pair of lips I've dreamed of my entire life.

Slowly, I lean forward, but my mouth barely brushes his before he pulls away. My heart aches at the rejection as Kolter rises to his full height and takes a step back.

"Stay safe, Peaches."

And with that, he moves back to his bike, slips on his helmet and fires off down the road, leaving me numb and embarrassed.

Chapter Eleven
Kolter

"Wake up, fucker!"

Those are the only words I hear before what feels like a goddamn elephant lands on me. I groan as I shove the person off me, causing them to crash to the floor, and slowly peel my eyes open. I ended up crashing at the clubhouse last night because I spent half the night circling Naomi's fucking block.

I knew she was safe; I knew that scumbag piece of shit from the club wasn't a threat, so I didn't stay close for her safety, like I usually do. No, this time, I stayed nearby because all I could think about was stomping up to her room, spreading her legs and sinking into her.

I circled that goddamn block until my arms were shaking from steering the bike.

I wipe the sleep from my eyes and sigh. I wish I'd never gone to that club. It's caused nothing but issues. Thoughts, desires, memories... everything I've been so desperate to escape. Everything I carefully tucked away in a box and shoved to the far recesses of my mind. They're all better off without me in their life, especially her. I know that—I get that. So I'm having trouble understanding just what the fuck I'm doing.

Ace hauls himself up off the ground, grimacing as he rubs the back of his head. "Christ, Blade. You're not very friendly in the morning. No wonder you can't keep a woman for longer than two minutes."

"No need for a woman past then," I scoff as I swing my legs round to the side of the bed and stand up.

Ace chuckles. "One day a good one is gonna come out of nowhere and knock you on your ass, and I'm gonna laugh the entire goddamn time."

I lift a challenging brow. "Want a bet on that?"

His face lights up with a grin. My friend, the perpetual gambler, can never turn down a bet.

"Hell yeah. Hm, let's see," he says as he strokes his chin with his finger. "If you make a woman your old lady by next Christmas, you owe me the Ducati."

"Fuck no," I spit. That thing is my baby. I have over a dozen bikes, but that one, absolutely not.

He smirks. "Come on. You're the one who hates women—this should be easy for you."

"If you lose, you're going to wash and polish it, weekly, until the end of time."

Ace balks at that. "I'm not sure those are fair terms."

"Who said they had to be fair?" I toss over my shoulder as I head for one of the bathrooms.

"Fuck, fine. I'm telling you, man. Your day of reckoning is coming, and I'm gonna look so good on the back of my new bike."

I roll my eyes, then head into the bathroom and start up the shower.

The hot water hits a tender spot on the back of my head, and I duck out of it for a moment before remembering where that came from. Last week, I got into a bar fight with another MC. Well, technically we all did. Some punk came up behind me and broke a bottle over the back of my head, but I stomped his teeth in, so really it was an eye for an eye and all that.

I can still hear Ace hooting and hollering down the hall, and it makes me sigh. I honestly don't know why I put up with him sometimes. I also don't know why I took the stupid bet. I mean, it's not like I think even for a second that I'm gonna lose. There's only one woman I've ever looked at in that way, and not only would it be wrong in the eyes of, well, everyone, she's the one person in the world I'd never involve in club business. Problem solved—insurance.

It still pisses me the fuck off that she got all dressed up—or in her case dressed down—and went out by herself last night. If I hadn't been watching over her, I don't even wanna think about what could have happened. She's so goddamn reckless, so glass half full when we live in a twisted and fucked-up world. She doesn't see it, though. Like an angel amongst us, she doesn't have a clue.

My cock twitches at the thought of her, the way that dress hugged every curve just right. The way her grey eyes shone the entire night. I've thought about taking her out for rides a lot in the past, but nothing could have prepared me for feeling her tight body pressed against my back, her arms clinging to me like I was her fucking lifeline.

Again, my cock jerks, and I grab hold of it, attempting to stop it. When I close my eyes, though, I see her, and I stroke my hand down my cock before sliding it back up. Fuck it. It's the closest I'll ever get to the real thing.

Slowly, I begin working my cock, thinking over every little detail of her last night. If I was just a slightly worse man, I would have followed her up into that room and taken her the way I've always desired. Is it fucked up to have dreamed of taking your adopted sister's virginity? Probably, though I never claimed to be holy.

She swallowed my cock so well in that club, and I'm desperate for that feeling again—her warm tongue wrapping around my head while I bury my hands in her golden hair. I'd let her set the speed at first, but by the end, I'd be fucking her face, and though she'd be choking on it, she'd love it even more than I would. She's a good girl, and good girls are always the best at getting dirty.

I feel my orgasm beginning to approach, so I stroke my cock faster and faster, imagining my hand is hers.

"Fuck," I mutter. "Peaches," I moan, and then I'm falling over the edge.

Wave after wave of pleasure slams into me as I grip the wall with my free hand to keep myself upright.

Once my orgasm has passed, though, guilt settles over me. I shouldn't have done that. I thought it would help, get her out of my system. Instead, I want her more than ever.

FUCK.

Chapter Twelve
Naomi

It's the first day back from spring break and I realize how much I missed school. That sounds weird, but honestly, I enjoy it. I like studying and learning. I've even debated going for a master's degree because I feel like there's so much more I want to learn. I'm definitely in the minority when it comes to that, though.

I'm one of the first students in the lecture hall for my first class, and I grab a spot off to the side, deciding to slide three seats in. Arianna and Cassi both take this class too, so I want to save them a seat. That is, if they still want to sit with me—though by *they*, I really mean Cassi. I haven't spoken to Arianna much since Cassi's birthday, honestly. She kinda went off the grid. Cassi, though, I'm dreading seeing.

Guilt gnaws at me as I think about our last conversation. I didn't mean to fly off the handle like that. I was drowning in conflicting feelings, disappointment and guilt, and I lashed out at the person closest to me in that moment. It sucks and it's a shit excuse, and I plan to apologize, if she's willing to hear me out.

As if my anxiety has summoned her, the door opens and she strides into the class, her red hair swaying behind her. She scans the room for a moment before her gaze lands on me. I wave, and she only hesitates for a second before heading towards me. That's a good sign, right?

When she reaches my row, she slides into the seat furthest from me, and I give her a meek smile.

"Hey."

A beat passes before she nods in response. "Hey."

She begins settling in, staring down at the paper in front of her, and doesn't say anything else.

Once the silence has reached an uncomfortable level, I ask, "How was your break?"

"Fine," Cassi says, turning to me. "You?"

"It was... interesting."

Interesting. That's a choice word. I feel like I'm starting to forget what life looked like before break started. Everything was different. Was it, though? Or did I make one huge mistake that turned into unresolved feelings I never got a chance to process, and now I'm sitting here trying to process them, but they're unrequited, so it's best that I suffer in silence, even though he knows how I feel about him and I swear he at least used to feel the same way about me but won't let himself admit it.

Phew.

Talk about an anxiety-fueled run-on sentence.

Cassi lifts a questioning brow, like she's trying to see if I'll elaborate. Fat chance of that. Maybe if things had gone differently... but no. I'm embarrassed, humiliated and ashamed that I'm lusting after my adopted brother and he doesn't even want me back. Forever that pathetic girl who doesn't belong—the one that gets the door slammed in her face. I'm an idiot, and I'd rather carry that shame in private.

Hoping to move the topic all the way off me, I face Cassi fully. "Are you still...?"

Her expression transforms into something dark.

"Sleeping with my sister's boyfriend? Yeah, I am," she snaps.

"That's what you really wanted to know, right? You want to bitch me out? Tell me what a horrible person I am some more? Go ahead, I'm ready for it," Cassi says, spreading her arms out as if to welcome my verbal blows.

Clearly, this isn't the time or place for this discussion as the class is growing fuller every second. So I shake my head and sigh, turning my attention to the syllabus agreement in front of me. I begin filling it out as Ari comes rushing into the room.

She quickly slips between Cassi and I, something I'm kinda grateful for.

"Dude, you live right across the street," Cassi scoffs. "How can you be the last person here?"

Ari looks around nervously and keeps her voice low. "Um, yeah. So I'm kind of not living there anymore."

"What do you mean?" I whisper.

Arianna licks her lips as her eyes move from Cassi's to mine. "I moved."

"Where?" Cassi asks.

"Now that everyone has finally joined us, we can get started," the professor says, shooting a pointed look at Arianna.

After the lecture, Arianna fills us in on what's been going on. She didn't hook up with just anyone at the club—she hooked up with her ex-stepdad. It was by accident at first, but then he followed her to her family's annual cabin trip and... now they're living together.

Shocked is the tamest word you could use for how Cassi and I both feel.

Honestly, I'm completely taken back. In a city filled with nearly a million people and an endless number of tourists, how is it possible that three of us can walk into a masked sex club, mess with three random strangers and somehow each of those strangers are some of the most inappropriate relationships possible?

Ari and her ex-stepdad.

Cassi and her sister's boyfriend.

Me and my brother.

What kind of fucked-up game is this, and why did we get picked as the unfortunate winners?

It's worse than just an accidental hookup. He and Ari are living together, so they're getting full-on serious, while Cassi has become a playboy's sidepiece, sneaking off to the other side of the country to drop her panties.

And me... I'm... Well, I guess nothing has really happened since that night. That moment in the driveway was one-sided, which means any inappropriate relations started and ended inside that club. Is it pathetic that I'm kind of jealous of my friends? I'm upset that despite how wrong it is, they seem... happy. Meanwhile, I'm over here, sullen and bitter. Why is that? Well, I think Cassi unfortunately might be on to something. I think this whole virginity thing is starting to eat away at my soul.

Finally, Cassi tells Ari we're happy for her, and I make sure my expression says I agree, though neither of them look totally convinced.

Then Ari turns the conversation round to us. "Whatever happened with you two that night?"

"Hm?" Cassi asks.

"I know you both hooked up. We've never shared details, though, which isn't like us. Now you know why I didn't share mine because, I mean, I wasn't exactly proud. Your turn bitches—spill."

I panic for a moment, not sure if I'm ready to fess up yet, and then my phone rings. It's just my mom, but I'll take any kind of distraction right now.

"Oh, got to take this. See you guys later!" I cry and quite literally run off.

"Hello?" I answer, once I'm far enough away.

"Hi, sweetie. Sorry to bother you. I just wanted to know what you'd like for dinner tonight?"

I can't help but laugh. "Anything is good with me, Mom."

It's been over two weeks since I've seen or heard from Kolter. Which isn't surprising, I suppose. I went years without seeing or hearing from him last time, so I think it's safe to say he's gone for good. Again.

Mom still watches the door at each family dinner, even after Nick's told her he isn't coming. I hate how much it hurts her that he chose his dad over her; that he chose people who turned their backs on him over his true family.

Cassi and I were able to make up. I apologized for how judgmental and out of line I was; she apologized for throwing my virginity in my face. Honestly, though, I don't blame her for doing so. I don't think it was just out of malice. She's on to something, and it's time I rip off the dang Band-Aid.

That's how I've ended up back at X—the elusive, brandless sex club that started all three of us down this journey. I didn't tell anyone I was coming. In hindsight, maybe that wasn't a great idea. Though this is much safer than going out downtown and possibly getting roofied, I still can't help but feel... nervous.

I stare at myself in the bathroom mirror, then close my eyes and blow out a deep breath. "You can do this. You are sexy, you are desired. Anyone would be happy to snatch your V-card off you. Tonight is the night."

Feeling more secure after my little pep talk, I wash my hands then slip out of the bathroom. There's an employee standing at the bottom of the stairs with a tablet in his hand who smiles at me when I make eye contact.

I do my best to hide the subtle shaking in my hands as I make my way towards him.

"Hi. Um, I was wondering where I could find a partner for, um, sex?"

Cringe. Could the ground maybe swallow me up now please?

The man smiles at me patiently. "I always suggest mingling at one of our many bars to ensure you make the right match. If you're looking for something a little less personal, though, you can simply step into one of our rooms and hang a colored card on the door handle. Silver means you're looking for a single partner. Gold means you're looking for many. Red is... well, I think you'll be set with silver or gold."

I nod. "And, um, where do I find these cards? And the rooms?" I wince. "Sorry."

He shakes his head and smiles as he gestures someone over. "Not a problem. Claudette will take you where you need to go. A private room please. One where she can invite a partner. Will you also show her the cards?"

"Of course." She smiles at me. "This way."

I follow the pretty woman up the stairs.

"Is this your first time here?" she asks.

"No, I just haven't done... this part before."

She looks back at me, attempting to conceal her smile. "Well, let me tell you, looking the way you do, I don't think you'll have any trouble at all finding a partner for the night."

Her tone is warm, encouraging. She basically just told me I'd have no problem getting laid in the same way a stranger would tell you they love your skirt. It's a little strange how different this world is, and I can't help but laugh.

When we reach the private rooms, Claudette opens an empty one for me and lets me inside.

Instantly, my jaw is on the floor. Holy moly. This is way nicer than the other rooms I experienced. Everything is luxe, leather and... posh? But like in a BDSM kind of way. It's hard to explain. I definitely didn't expect anything near this nice.

I turn to Claudette. "Who pays for all of this?" I ask.

"Hm?"

"The rooms, the entertainment. I haven't been asked to pay for a thing besides drinks both times I've been inside. I can't help but wonder who funds this place."

She smiles. "Our paying members get exclusive benefits—that more than covers things. And the rest of our clientele find us through word of mouth, so that keeps things exclusive."

I nod and look around the room in awe.

"Over here are your cards. What are you looking for tonight?"

"Um, just one please."

She grabs the silver card from the wall. "I'll put this one up for you. Relax, make yourself comfortable, and if you need anything, security is just outside these doors."

"Thank you," I say.

She smiles and slips out of the room, leaving the door halfway open —I assume so people can peek in and decide if they like what they see?

For a moment, I just stand awkwardly in the middle of the room, resting my hand onto my hip. Then I choose to sit on the edge of the bed. Should I lie down? Look inviting? What's a pose that says, *This V-card isn't gonna swipe itself?*

A few people walk past, poking their heads in curiously before going on their way, and my disappointment grows with each one. What if I'm not good enough? What if no one picks me? What if I strip down naked, dip myself in a vat of oil and I'm still not sexy enough for anyone to want to screw me?

I lower my head, about to accept defeat, when the door is pushed fully open. I look up to see a handsome man with strawberry-blonde hair and a black mask. He's wearing a crisp black jacket and matching slack with a white undershirt. His eyes roam over me for a moment before a smile lights up his face.

"Mind if I join you?" he asks.

Hope begins to bloom inside me. I could definitely do worse.

I wave him inside. "Please."

Please? Really, Nay?

He grins then snatches the silver card off the handle before shutting the door with a resounding thud.

His eyes never leave mine as he swaggers across the room. My heart is beating in my chest like a drum, and there's a lump lodged firmly in my throat, no matter how hard I try to swallow it down.

When he reaches me, he hesitates for a moment before gently cupping my chin. "What do you like?" he asks.

"I... I don't know. I've never... This is my first..." I trail off.

Excitement lights up his features. "Relax, I'll take great care of you."

I nod as he slips his hand up to cradle my face, pulling me towards him for a kiss. I sink into it, my stomach flipping at the contact. His tongue pushes into my mouth almost all at once. It's a little much, but I adjust to it and tangle my tongue around his.

Slowly, he pushes me backward onto the bed, covering my body with his as he begins peppering my neck with kisses. I'm buzzing with nerves, adrenaline and I think a little bit of euphoria. Everything feels so good. I can't believe I waited so long to do this. And for what? I've never had a good reason. It just never felt right. But I can tell you, in this moment, everything feels just right. Great, even.

Layer by layer, he strips down before peeling off my dress and panties until I'm left in only my heels. Then the man grabs my leg, running his tongue down my calf to my shoe.

Okay, a little odd, but I'm gonna roll with it.

"Fuck! How is this your first time? Look at you!" he says reverently. "Can't wait to eat this pussy."

I smile shyly and shrug as he crawls in between my legs, burying his face between my thighs before his tongue licks through me.

"Oh my God!" I say, my hips bucking against him.

He licks through me again and again. It feels a little probing at first, but when his tongue slides over my clit, a moan escapes me that has him grinning.

"You like that, princess?"

"Princess?" I question.

He smiles. "You look like a princess from one of my daughter's movies."

Something about that sentence rubs me the wrong way, but I do my best to ignore it. Closing my eyes, I force myself to be in the moment. To enjoy this.

His tongue wiggles through me a few times, stroking against my clit occasionally. I'm so close—all I need is him to focus a little more on my clit and it's straight to orgasm town for me. Is it rude if I give him pointers, though? Will he be offended?

Whatever. I'm sure it'll be fine.

When he runs his tongue against my clit again, I grind myself against his face, and he seems to get the hint. My eyes roll into the back of my head as my orgasm starts creeping in

And then another body touches the bed.

My eyes fly open, and there's Kolter standing before me. No mask, just a look of fury on his face.

Before I can even process what's happening, he's jammed a knife into the back of the guy's neck, pushing it up with such force that his head drops instantly, blood already drenching the bed.

My mouth drops as I look at the scene in front of me with wide eyes.

Oh my God.

Oh my God.

I... I think he's dead.

Chapter Thirteen
Kolter

I look down at the motionless piece of shit before me—he's soaking the bed and filling the room with that familiar scent of iron. Naomi is staring down at him in horror, shaking slightly. If I was a better person, I'd maybe care about traumatizing her like this.

Truth be told, I didn't show up intent on killing someone. I've been keeping tabs on her, and when I saw her walk into my club—alone at that—I knew I had to find out what she was up to. It took just one conversation with one of my employees to find her, and when I discovered the door was already closed, anger like I've never felt before surged through me. I didn't think—I acted. Just like right the fuck now.

I shove the body to the floor. The blood from his entry wound starts seeping into the carpet, but he's the least of my concerns right now.

I lift a blood-stained hand and squeeze Naomi's cheeks together. "This is your fault," I snarl. "You get that? His death—it's on YOU."

She blinks up at me a few times, almost like she doesn't really see me, then shakes her head—as much as she can anyway.

"H-How? You're the one who k-killed him."

"No," I grit, bringing my face to hers.

My nose presses against the bridge of hers as I speak, ensuring each syllable cuts like a knife.

"You let him in. You spread your legs. You were ready to hand over something that has always been—and will always be—*mine*."

"What?" she asks breathlessly.

I'm fucking done talking, though.

I shove her onto her back and climb onto the bed, pushing her legs up until she's fully exposed for me, then pull my cock out of my pants. It's fucking pulsating at this point because... fuck, look at her. She's perfect, even more perfect than I ever imagined.

"You're so desperate to get rid of your virginity? Fine. Consider it gone."

Without a second of hesitation or warning, I slam into her. She lets out a pained cry that I can feel in my soul, but I close my eyes and grit my teeth, not allowing myself to feel it. All I can focus on is her and... Jesus fucking Christ do I feel her. I feel the moment I tear through her hymen; I feel the wetness of her pussy combined with her virgin blood. It makes my cock throb inside her, and I push even deeper, until she's practically crawling up the wall.

I draw back almost completely which I can tell gives her a small amount of relief as her bright eyes meet mine.

"Congratulations, Peaches—you're no longer a goddamn virgin."

With that, I begin thrusting. She screeches and gasps for air, limply pushing against me. It's like her body wants me to stop, but something else inside her doesn't. She never says no, never begs for me to stop. She just grunts and squirms like she's working through the pain.

Gripping her hips in my hands, I pick up my speed, staring down at her and shaking my head. This is not how I pictured this, ever, and fucking trust me: I've pictured taking my sister's virginity countless times. Goddamn, that sounds even more twisted than the reality of it.

I imagined her gifting me her virginity. A raw and intense

moment just for the two of us, where we'd come together, and I'd show her all the ways I would love and care for her. It would be soft and gentle, everything she'd ever hoped.

Instead, here I am, violently fucking her in a sex club in a pool of her almost-hookup's blood while his corpse cools on the floor beneath us. It's less than perfect; it's not a moment to be shared by two lovers. It fits, though. Those fantasies were for a different time, a different man. One that I couldn't afford to be, not even for her.

I hope she hates me after this. I hope she never wants to look me in the eyes again. It will make what comes next much easier.

But I know it won't be that simple. My... temper has just made everything that much more complicated, and now she's involved, whether I want her to be or not.

My orgasm begins to build, and selfishly I ride it out, giving not a single thought to her pleasure. It's easier this way—it has to be like this. I lose myself in wave after wave of euphoria, my cum filling her cunt until I have nothing left to give.

No matter how desperately I want to collapse onto her, curl into this bed and begin atoning for all the wrongs I've done, including this one, I don't. Instead, I blow out a short breath and push myself to my feet, pulling out of her without another second of hesitation.

She looks up at me, tears pouring down her face as I stare down at her before shifting my gaze to the body on the floor. Then I reach into my pants, fish out my phone, and make a call.

"Hey, it's me. Bring a clean-up crew to the club. We've had an incident."

Chapter Fourteen
Naomi

Kolter barely lets me get dressed before he's dragging me out of that room. I feel... sticky. From the man's blood, from Kolter's cum... I'm not sure which is more prominent.

He hauls me through the club by the arm then shoves me through a side door into what looks like a service elevator. A heavy sense of dread fills me as he punches one of the buttons and the elevator begins taking us down.

My body is shaking—I think mainly from shock. I'm having difficulty understanding everything that just happened. I mean, I lived it, but I also sort of didn't. It was like I was an observer, watching everything occur. One moment, I was ready to have a no-strings-attached hookup to rid myself of my virginity once and for all, the next Kolter is killing the man and tearing me in half while he claims my virginity for himself.

You were ready to hand over something that has always been—and will always be—mine.

His words echoed in my head the entire time. Each thrust seemed more punishing than the last, like he was trying to hurt me. Physically, yes, he absolutely met the mark. Emotionally? He never could. Not when real truths like that bubble from his lips before he's able to stop them.

Despite the pleasure he took in the act, I know Kolter Mayhew better than anyone in the world. Better than he knows himself, I'd guess. It doesn't matter that he's been gone for years; it doesn't matter that he's involved in this... gang, or whatever. He will always be my Kolter, and I'll always be his Peaches. He made that abundantly clear tonight.

The question is, how far is he willing to go to prove me wrong? That thought alone is the cause of the growing knots in my stomach.

After all, he killed a man right in front of me. No hesitation. No regret. I have no doubt it wasn't the first time, and I'm sure it won't be the last. If I was smarter, I'd be terrified that I was about to meet the same fate, but I know that's a line he could never cross. Then again, maybe I'm holding a little too much faith for the boy I knew instead of the man before me.

When the elevator doors open, we step through a back room then out into an alley, where Kolter's bike is ready and waiting. He grabs the helmet off the handlebar and slams it down on my head before swinging his leg over his bike and firing it up. I hesitate for a moment before I realize that he won't wait for me.

Quickly, I jump onto the back of the bike and wrap my arms around his waist before he tears out of the alley and merges onto the main road. This isn't a soft and easy ride like before. He's unleashing the throttle, leaning into turns so deeply I feel like we're going to crash. The thrill I felt during that first ride has been obliterated, replaced by fear of the unknown.

Kolter navigates us through town for what feels like ever before he pulls up to a run-down-looking bar. Or is it a saloon? Do those only exist in old western movies? Whatever it is, it looks like the kind of place where a bunch of old cowboys would go for their whisky. Or, based on the number of motorcycles out front, a bunch of bikers.

Kolter kills the engine and jumps off the bike, then pulls me down next to him, grabs the helmet off my head and tosses it to the ground before dragging me up the front steps and into the bar.

The smell of stale beer and cheap liquor hits me, and I can't help but wrinkle my nose. All eyes swing to us as Kolter hauls me through the bar, his boots thundering against the wooden floors. Men dressed in matching leather cut-off jackets and riding pants all watch me carefully, while several women barely wearing enough to cover their nips and slits shoot daggers at me with their eyes—especially one woman with bright-red hair.

"Blade, what's going on?" a guy asks.

He looks familiar, and it takes me a moment to place him. The club. That first night. After the... glory hole.

What was his name again? Axle? Arson?

"Not now, Ace," Kolter snarls before tugging me into a back hallway.

He kicks open a door then shoves me through the gap onto the single bed in the middle of the room. The door slams shut, and I hear the sound of a key turning in a lock.

Panic fills me as I rush to the door and try the knob, but sure enough, he's locked me in.

What the heck?

I look around the windowless room, trying to work through my options, and then the door reopens. Relief fills me as Kolter steps inside.

"What's going on? Where are we?" I ask.

"Where's your phone?" he asks shortly, moving towards me.

I frown. "My phone? I-I don't know. Back at the club, I think. Crap, so is my purse."

I shake my head, trying to gain some perspective as I stare at Kolter. "What's going on? Are you, like, holding me hostage or some-thing?" I throw out, mostly kidding.

When he doesn't smile or smirk, that heavy feeling of dread drops into my stomach once more.

"Until further notice. Don't try to run—you won't make it."

The emotional whiplash has my head spinning. What the hell is happening? Is this not the same man that tore through my virginity like it was his lifelong destiny to do so? Is this not the boy I've loved all my life?

"Kolt," I whisper.

He tenses for a moment, his jaw tightening as he shakes his head. "Don't."

Then he turns on his heel and slams the door shut behind him—so hard the walls shake—before locking it once more.

Kolter's voice grows quieter as he moves away, but I do hear him shout at someone to watch the door.

I'm left standing there in a daze of confusion.

Did I just get kidnapped?

Chapter Fifteen
Kolter

"You gonna tell me what's going on?" Ace asks, trying to keep up with me.

"Wasn't planning on it," I snap as I head back out to my bike.

I don't want to leave her here, but I don't have a choice. I have to figure out how to keep her from running her mouth to the cops. I don't think she'd narc, not on me at least, but I can't risk it. So she's gonna stay at the clubhouse until I can work out what the fuck to do with her.

Goddamnit.

I rake my fingers through my hair then step out onto the front porch and aim a kick at one of the wooden chairs there. Unsatisfied by the mere inches it moves, I lift it over my head and smash it into the ground. What the fuck have I done? What was I thinking?

That's the problem. I *wasn't* fucking thinking. I was acting—or reacting—and now I'm fucked.

"Jesus, Blade. You gotta tell me what's happening. I can help," Ace insists.

I turn to him, my eyes no doubt filled with the rage I feel, and snarl, "I killed a guy back at the sex club, and she saw me do it. I gotta deal with clean-up and figure out how to make her keep her mouth shut, and I need it all done before Snakes comes round. Can you help with any of that?"

Ace looks surprised. "Who did you take out? How did she see? Have you called a clean-up crew yet?"

"Yes," I huff. "They should be there now, but I need someone to supervise. Pay off the staff, erase the security footage."

Ace nods. "I can take care of all of that."

Sometimes, I forget how helpful this fucker can be. He's dumber than a box of rocks at times but he'd do anything for this club, anything for me.

I shake my head, letting out an aggravated sigh. "I fucked up."

Ace stays quiet for a few moments. Then he says, "That's the girl from the club a while back, yeah?"

Slowly, I lift my gaze to him. I don't respond—I don't need to. He can read the answer on my face.

He nods then claps me on the shoulder. "You take care of your girl; I'll handle the rest."

"She's not my girl," I snap.

Ace lifts a disbelieving brow then heads towards his bike. "I'll let you know when it's taken care of."

I don't say thanks. I don't need to, and he doesn't expect it.

Dutifully, Ace climbs onto his bike and roars off towards town. He's the only one I'd trust to handle a mess like this. Typically, I'd manage it all, but I have other issues to deal with right now.

When I push my way back inside, several curious gazes meet mine, but none of them dare say a word—except one obnoxious fuck.

Fire Crotch steps in front of me and rests her hand on my chest. "Where you going, baby? You look stressed. Let me relax you."

I don't even look at her; I just grab her shoulders and shove her back towards Tank, who already has his dick in his hand, ready and waiting for her. He catches her easily and smiles while she tosses me a venomous glare.

She really shouldn't fucking push me. I've already killed once tonight—another body or two means nothing to me at this point.

I stomp through the bar to the back of the clubhouse, where Brick is standing guard outside Naomi's room.

"She's a fiery one. Been beating the hell out of the door," Brick says with a smirk.

I roll my eyes and shoo him away before unlocking the door and pushing it open.

Naomi hasn't realized she has company yet. No, she's too busy trying to pry up a loose board from the floor. She's almost got it too, then she loses her grip and it snaps back into place.

"Cheese on a freaking cracker," she snaps.

"What exactly are you planning to do with that thing?" I ask stiffly.

She jumps and climbs to her feet. "Nothing. I don't know. I was preparing."

"For?" I ask sharply.

"I don't know. It kinda feels like I'm going to be interrogated or beaten. Maybe even stabbed in the back of the neck. Didn't want any of that to happen without a fighting chance."

My eyes roam over her scantily clad body, taking in those thin arms I could break with a flick of my wrist and those pretty, pouty eyes that have always been too clear and too innocent. Like they've never seen a single horror in all their days. She's pure, untouched by the hell that is this world. Or she was until tonight.

Frustration, anger, desire, need—it all swarms inside me, each feeling desperate to claim center stage. I'm losing control again, quickly. Just like before, all rational thought is flying out the window, leaving only instinct in its place, and if I continue to allow it, there will be no saving either of us.

My gaze pauses between her legs. There's a small red spot smeared on her upper thigh. It's not a lot, but it's enough to have me frowning.

"Is that his blood?" I ask.

She looks down at her blood-stained hands before her eyes move to where mine rest.

"I don't know," she whispers.

Jesus fucking Christ.

I reach for her, and she startles back—but not quickly enough. My hand wraps around her arm, and I pull her out into the hallway then along it until I reach one of the main bathrooms.

I slam on the shower, turning the water as hot as it'll go before kicking the bathroom door shut. When I face her, I find she's watching me with caution. I fucking hate that look. It's not one I'm familiar with, not on her at least. Something about it pisses me the fuck off.

I push her into the shower so the warm water is pouring over her, clothes and all. She gasps at the shock of it, and I follow her, closing the glass door behind us before backing her up against the wall. Water cascades over the both of us, smearing her makeup as I brace my hands above her head and... breathe. Well, I try to breathe. It's more like I'm raggedly blowing air into her face. I can't catch my breath; I can't get a bit of oxygen. All I feel is... too fucking much.

"Kolt," Naomi says softly, in a way that tugs at a part of me I thought had died long ago.

"Don't," I say, though I'm more begging at this point.

Begging because I can't be held responsible for any of my actions tonight. I can't be held responsible for any future actions if she keeps looking at me like this, talking to me like this, being like... this.

"It's okay," she coos softly, like I'm the one that needs to be talked the fuck down.

Do you believe this girl?

"It's not!" I argue as my fist slams into the wall beside her head.

She doesn't flinch, doesn't even blink. Instead, she just nods and says in that same gentle tone, "It's okay. I'm okay; you're okay."

A bitter laugh escapes me as I drop my gaze to the floor, shaking with rage. "Nothing is fucking okay, Peaches. I've spent the last six years of my life keeping my distance, making sure you were nowhere near this place. I didn't want you involved; I still don't, and yet here you fucking are." I laugh, though there's not an ounce of humor in my goddamn tone.

"Then let me go," she says simply.

"What?" I snarl, whipping my head so I can look into her eyes.

"I won't tell anyone, ever. You know that. Even if you try to convince yourself I'm a liability, you know I'd never do anything to get you in trouble. So you don't have to keep me prisoner or... whatever it is you're doing. You can let me go. You can disappear again. I'll never see you or hear from you. Things can go back to how they were, if you want."

She swallows roughly, like her next words are harder to get out.

"All you have to do," she continues, "is let me go."

I feel numb. From the top of my head, down to my fingers and toes, and every inch of me in between. Her words float in the air between us, heavy, full of promise. It would be easy to agree. To take her back to her side of town, drop her at her doorstep and never look back.

But I've done that. I've been there.

And look where it's left me.

The realization that I'm no longer in charge hits me like a ton of bricks. I'm spiraling. Out of control, out of my goddamn mind. I know there's no stopping it, though.

Tightening my hands into fists beside her head, I slowly lower my face to hers as my tone takes on a vicious edge.

"No."

Chapter Sixteen
Naomi

I don't have a chance to process Kolter's one simple word before his lips are on mine. The air is snatched from my lungs, my stomach does a dozen summersaults, and I feel as if my entire body is floating in the air, all at once. Come to think of it, that last part is true —Kolter's arms are beneath my legs, and he has me lifted into the air, my back pressed against the shower wall as his lips move down my neck.

"Kolt," I rasp, wrapping my arms around his neck.

He groans like he's in pain as he tears his mouth away from my skin, pausing when our faces are just a hair's breadth away from one another.

"You don't know how long I've dreamed of you saying my name in that way."

If it's at all possible, right in this moment, I love him more now than ever before. Is it love or lust? Maybe it doesn't have to be an either/or. I've loved this man practically my whole life, I've wanted him for almost as long, and now... I'm... here. As easy as it would be to overanalyze every detail, every word, every gesture, I push all my thoughts to the side and instead choose to just... feel.

My fingers fist into the back of his hair as I drag him towards me once more. This time, when our mouths meet, I trace the seam of his lips with my tongue before his own tangles around mine. He presses me harder against the wall, freeing one of his hands so it can move all over my body. It's like we can't get enough of one another—as if our hands need to double and triple check that this is actually real, that we're really in front of each other. That this is happening.

I reach for the back of his shirt—now so soaked it's like a second skin—ball the material into my hands, then begin dragging it up and over his head. He puts some space between us, setting me down for a moment so he can help with the shirt before grabbing the hem of my dress. Then he strips the soggy material off my body and tosses it to the floor, where it lands with a wet slap.

Kolter's fingers effortlessly release the clasp of my bra then slide the straps down so it falls away. His last target is my panties, though it's not like they're covering much. Certainly nothing he hasn't already seen, though you wouldn't know it by the way he's looking at me.

He stares at me with such reverence, like I'm the eighth wonder of the world. Like I'm the greatest art he's ever seen. The power it gives me is unlike anything I've ever experienced. It's addictive, intoxicating, and I suddenly crave to be marveled at like this for all my days.

Kolter hooks his thumbs into the waistband of my panties, working them down my legs before letting them fall to the floor. He lowers himself with them, pausing when his face is level with the apex of my thighs. Slowly, he lifts one of my legs and wraps it around his shoulder before nuzzling his face against the crease in my thigh and inhaling.

I shudder at the feel of his breath on my skin, goosebumps racing across my body as that cool gaze meets my own. Without breaking our eye contact, he flattens his tongue and slowly licks through me.

The sensation has me bucking against him and a moan tearing out of my chest.

I don't know if the others can hear me. We aren't exactly alone in this place, so I should try to be at least a little discreet. When Kolter does it again and again, though, I know there's no concealing anything. I'm a goner for Kolter Mayhew, and I don't care who knows it.

He expertly works me over with his tongue, licking and sucking in just the right way and leaving me a shaking mess. One of my hands reaches down, for stability I think, and fists his thick black hair. He moans in response and buries his face deeper between my thighs, his mouth latching on to my clit. My mouth drops open, and then with another pass of his tongue, I'm splintering apart.

"Oh my God! Oh! Oh!" I scream, covering my mouth as my orgasm slams into me like an uncontrollable freight train.

As my pleasure eases, Kolter pulls his mouth away and stands slowly, his eyes staying on me as he rises to his full height. My breathing is still ragged as I attempt to recover—though how do I recover from something like... that?

For a moment, I'm not sure what his next move will be. He's the most unpredictable man in the most predictable circumstances, so all I can do is breathe and watch.

Kolter's expression is practically undecipherable as his eyes flick back and forth between mine. Then he lifts a hand, gently cupping my cheek before bringing his lips to mine once more. It's not an impassioned, hurried kiss like before. It's not a result of years of tension breaking down into one moment of acceptance. It's soft, tender, so featherlight I almost think I imagine it.

His lips ghost over my own as he rests his forehead against mine. "That should have been our first moment. The first time I touched you, it should have felt like that."

My heart squeezes in my chest, and I do my best to steady my voice.

"It was perfect. Both times. Every time," I ramble breathlessly like an idiot.

He doesn't look at me like I'm one, though. No matter how quirky or awkward I feel, Kolter has always looked at me as if I hung the moon and the stars. He listens like every word I speak is the next great epic. Like my every thought is the answer our world has been desperate for. It's an incredibly comforting feeling that I didn't know I missed so much. It's more than being cared for, deeper than affection. With him, it's something else entirely.

His arms slip beneath my legs once, then he lifts me into the air and begins walking us out of the shower. He doesn't reach for a towel despite his water-logged pants dripping profusely. He doesn't even attempt to grab anything to cover me. Instead, he opens the bathroom door, turns so that I'm completely hidden from anyone who might be in the hallway then moves into a different bedroom than the one we were in earlier.

Kolter kicks the door shut behind us before carrying me to the bed. He pulls the blankets back, sets me down carefully, then shucks off his soaked shoes, pants and boxers and climbs in beside me. I expect there to be more kissing or touching; I'm preparing my extremely sore vagina for the reality of a round two. But none of it happens.

Instead, we just lie there, me wrapped up in Kolter's embrace, which is so tight I couldn't move an inch if I tried.

I don't know how long we lie there in silence before I finally look up to find him frowning at the blank wall.

"What's wrong?" I ask.

He snaps free of whatever deep thoughts were plaguing him and presses a kiss to my forehead. "Nothing. It's just... you shouldn't be here. I shouldn't have brought you here. I shouldn't have gone to the club. I've tried for so long to keep you and our family safe. Away from all this," he says, gesturing around the room. "Yet here we are." He lets out a raspy laugh that holds no humor.

I ready myself for the blow that's sure to come. "So you don't want me here?" I ask tentatively.

"No," he answers quickly.

Is it stupid that my throat is already tightening and my eyes are beginning to blur with unshed tears? I accepted his rejection years ago; I coped and moved on, though the circumstances were much different then. Years ago, he ghosted our family; slipped away into the night without a word, but now I know what it feels like to be held by him. To be kissed, touched. And I have a feeling the recovery process won't be the same at all. Though, if I'm being honest, I'm not sure it's possible to recover from a heartbreak like this.

His large hand cups my face, forcing me to look at him. "I love you, Peaches. I've loved you before I even understood what that word meant. I stayed away for years because I thought it was what was best."

I swallow roughly and nod.

"I can't do it anymore, though. I don't want to. A life without you isn't one worth living. So even if it's the most selfish goddamn thing I've ever done in my life, I'm not walking away again. Ever."

It takes me a moment to comprehend his words.

"You mean it?" I whisper, like a pleading hope.

"With my last breath," he vows, his words inking their way into my soul.

Chapter Seventeen
Naomi

The morning sun is streaming through the window, a stale, unfamiliar scent filling my nose. I open my eyes slowly, trying to get my bearings. Where am I?

A soft exhale from a bare chest beneath me has all my memories flooding back. Every breath, touch and feeling buries me—until I blink out of it and meet Kolter's sleepy gaze.

"What's wrong?" he rumbles, his voice rough.

"Nothing. I just... I was trying to figure out if everything from last night was a dream or not."

He tilts his head to the side in curiosity and maybe a touch of amusement.

"Like the club," I say. "And the... guy. You... removing him. Then..." I swallow. "And then back here, and all the things we said to each other after we—"

Kolter leans forward, squeezing my cheeks in one of his hands as he presses his lips to mine.

Okay. Confirmed. Definitely not a dream. All of it, definitely real.

Holy moly.

"You know, Peaches. I get that you were a sweet virgin about twelve hours ago, but you better get used to talking about the way I fuck you into oblivion because it's gonna keep happening."

"It is?" I ask, not even attempting to keep the hopeful lilt from my voice.

A crooked smirk lifts one side of his mouth before he places a quick kiss on my forehead. "Yes. A lot. I'm giving you the day to recover, but that's all I'm giving you."

"I'm fine," I say quickly, causing him to laugh and shake his head.

Slowly, Kolter untangles himself from the bed and pushes to stand. He's completely naked, and in the light of day, I can't help but admire his bare butt as he slides on his boxers and jeans—more or less dry now. My God. Men are blessed with being pretty enough not to need makeup and they also have better butts than us? Where is the justice in the world?

He rifles through his drawers before tossing me a pair of black sweatpants and a T-shirt. "Here, put these on."

"Why?" I ask, peeling the covers away from me and sliding out of bed.

Kolter's gaze moves to me, his eyes slowly raking over me from head to toe, a lustful haze clouding his features before he shakes his head and curses under his breath.

"Because if you go out there in your 'come fuck me' little black dress, I'm gonna have to kill every last goddamn man in this MC."

I can't help but flush. "It wasn't a come... F me dress," I mutter in defense.

Kolter finishes pulling on his own T-shirt then closes the distance between us. "Trust me, Peaches, that's the signal you were sending. That's why a man is dead this morning and you're in bed with me instead of tucked back home."

My eyes widen. "He's dead?"

Kolter scoffs like I just made a joke, but when he sees the look on my face, he frowns. "I thought you knew."

I did. Deep down. There was too much blood. He went too still. I knew Kolter didn't call 911 or have a medical team rush to his aid. Of course he was dead. Still, hearing it—hearing him say that it was my fault—unsettles me.

"So, I killed a man?" I ask tightly.

What looks like empathy crosses his face before Kolter cups the back of my head in his hands. "No, Peaches, I did. I killed him for touching my girl."

"But I wasn't—"

His finger comes to my lips, freezing them in place as he levels me with a hard look. "Are you honestly going to lie to me and tell me that you haven't been mine since the moment I set eyes on you? That I haven't been yours in return?"

"I..."

That's all I can manage to say. That's all I can manage to think because what the hell else am I supposed to think or say when this man is telling me all the things I used to dream about? And now he's here, in front of me, melting me in my place.

Kolter reaches for the shirt and sweatpants, then slides both onto me—dropping a few kisses against my skin along the way—before rising to his full height once more.

"I'm going to talk to one of my guys, and then we're going to leave. I'll take you to breakfast and then take you home, okay?"

I smile softly. "Okay."

Kolter's fingers intertwine with mine, sending my heart skipping a beat like I'm a lovesick teenager and we're walking the school halls for the first time as an official couple. How stupid am I?

When Kolter pulls the door open, the air around us instantly shifts, like the safe, warm cocoon we've been wrapped in for the last few hours has been snatched away, leaving us cast adrift in the early-morning chill.

In just a few feet, we're through the hallway and into the main bar area, which means it takes no time to have what feels like a hundred pairs of eyes on us. Okay, that's a gross exaggeration; there are maybe twenty people in the place. Still, though—the feeling instantly puts me on edge and has me wanting to shrink behind Kolter.

He seems to sense my unease and stands a little taller, blocking me from the onlookers.

"Got a new toy, Blade?" a man calls over. Half of his teeth are missing, and the other half are rotted black.

The way he smiles at me sends goosebumps running up and down my spine, but they're quickly chased away by Kolter's snarl.

"I'll pluck your goddamn eyes from your head if you look at her again—that's a fucking promise."

The man seems to take his threat seriously, quickly averting his gaze to the beer in front of him as Kolter begins moving forward, keeping his hand in mine.

We stop at a table with a tall, wide man maybe ten years older than Kolter and a woman. She has long hair and more tattoos and piercings than I can count. She also has an extremely kind smile—a knowing one like she understands how... uncomfortable this situation is for me.

"Stay with her. I'll be a minute," Kolter says.

The woman smiles and nods, scooting over to make room for me in the booth. I glance up at Kolter cautiously, and he gives me a quick, encouraging nod.

Slowly, I take a seat beside the woman, and the man stands up, moving to sit on the other side of me. I jolt in surprise, but he lifts his hands in the air to demonstrate his innocence.

"Easy, darlin'. I'm just sitting here so one of these pukes don't," he says, jutting his chin towards the room full of men who are still watching me like I'm a steak dinner.

"He looks like a big brute, and he is, but he'll keep you safe. Boss's orders and all," the woman beside me teases.

"Kolter is the boss?" I ask, turning towards her.

"Blade?" she asks. "I mean, sort of. He's the boss's son, the future heir and all that, and he's got a nasty temper."

I furrow my brows and look over to Kolter, who's now in the corner with a familiar-looking guy. It takes me a moment to place him before I realize he's the guy who guarded my door last night; who was with Kolter in the club that first night. The way they're talking, they're clearly friends. Both of their faces are pinched and serious, though, and the guy occasionally glances towards me, putting me instantly on edge.

"So, where did you meet Blade?" the woman asks.

I tear my gaze away from Kolter and turn to her. "What?"

She smiles patiently. "Where did you meet him? You don't look like a typical cut slut."

Her eyes rake over me, but not in a judgmental way—more like she's appraising me. Understandable considering I'm drowning in Kolter's clothes.

"Uh, we grew up together," I say, hoping that's okay to say.

It's not the full truth, but it's not a lie either. We did grow up together.

Just in the same house.

"Really? That's cool. Brick and I have been together since I was in high school."

He nods. "That's right."

"Yep, I jumped on the back of his bike and never looked back. I mean, after I found out how hung he was."

A choked laugh escapes Brick, and my eyes widen in surprise.

"Christ, Star. Think you're gonna scare the poor girl."

Star gives me a wicked smile before bumping my shoulder. "She survived the night with Blade—she can take it."

A memory tugs inside my head. One I struggle to place.

"Star?" I ask.

She smiles. "That's me."

It takes me another few seconds—then my eyes widen, and my back goes rigid.

She watches me curiously, her smile slowly falling. "You okay?"

"Yeah, I just... Um. Have you ever been to the club downtown? The—"

"Sex one?" she fills in. "Yeah, I mean the club owns it. We all go all the time. Why do you ask—"

Her words stall as she studies me. Then, without warning, she reaches over and runs her fingers through my hair, startling me. Then she smacks the table and shouts, "Holy shit! Brick! This is our mystery girl!"

"What?" he asks, leaning forward to look at his girl before turning to me.

"Instantly, I thought your voice was familiar, but I couldn't place it. Oh my God. The one time I wished we weren't in the dark room. How have you been, baby?" she says, her smile turning a touch seductive she continues playing with my hair.

I swallow awkwardly as Kolter and his friend come over to the table.

"What's going on?" Kolter asks, looking at me as if checking I'm okay.

"We just made a little discovery. Seems we got there before you, Blade," Star says, curling her arm round my shoulder. "Brick and I had a little playtime with this one in the dark room several weeks back. Might just have to fight you for her. That mouth..." she says, biting her lower lip and shaking her head.

"He touched you?" Kolter asks stiffly.

I look to him nervously, not sure what to say. "Um, a little, kinda."

There's no hesitation, not a single moment of delay before Kolter drives his fist into Brick's face. Brick's hand flies to his mouth to staunch the blood that starts flowing immediately.

"Why did you do that?" I ask, shocked.

"So I could help wash the taste of you out of his mouth," Kolter growls, keeping his eyes on Brick.

"In my defense, she was way more into Star than me," Brick tosses back.

Kolter's eyes cut to Star, who rolls her eyes.

"What? You gonna hit me too? Calm down—it was forever ago."

Kolter's chest is heaving as he attempts to control his anger. He reaches for me, wrapping his hand around my arm and yanking me to my feet. I stumble towards him, but he catches me easily, cupping my face then smashing his mouth against my own in a punishing kiss.

It's filled with rage, but slowly gives way to passion. Before I can fully sink into him, though, he tears his mouth away, tucks me into his side then glowers down at them both.

"Either one of you touches my woman again, I'll fucking bury you."

Brick nods like he understands, while Star just rolls her eyes again and mutters, "You're no fucking fun."

Brick knocks his boot against hers, silently telling her to shut it. She gives Kolter a fake salute, but he just turns and starts leading me towards the door.

Then he stops.

An older man steps through the doorway. He's tall, with dirty blonde hair that's giving way to white and a long scraggly beard. The scars and wrinkles on his face suggest he's in his sixties at least—or maybe he's younger and has just lived a rough life. Either way, his dark eyes are heavy, and they move from me to Kolter with precision.

"Where you going?" the gruff man asks Kolter.

"Gonna take her home, then go deal with some business at the club."

The man scoffs and shakes his head. "I know all about your business at the club. Been on the phone with a detective for the last hour keeping them off our fucking ass."

Kolter's brow furrows. "What? How? It's been cleaned up. It was taken care of. Ace?" Kolter says, turning to his friend.

Ace nods. "I oversaw it myself."

"What you dipshits didn't oversee is the fucking busboy across the street. Saw a body loaded up into a car and our guys follow said car."

Kolter's expression turns stoic. His next words are tight, his voice low. "Does he know?"

"No, not yet."

The man's eyes move to mine slowly before he shakes his head and looks back to Kolter. "Care to explain?"

He nods. "I'm gonna run her home, then I'll be back."

"That's not what I fucking said. Now," he demands, pushing past us and stomping through the bar to the back.

"Fuck," Kolter curses under his breath. "I gotta handle this. Ace, will you take her home?"

"Of course. Hi," he greets me, smiling gently like he's worried he's going to frighten me.

He's not as tattooed as all the others, just a scattering of ink on his arms, and definitely not as old either, probably in between Kolter's age and mine. He has mousy brown hair, a thick matching beard and a single eyebrow piercing.

"Hi," I say softly.

Kolter drops his mouth to my ear, placing a gentle, unnoticeable kiss there. "He'll get you home safe. I'll come by tonight for dinner. Wait for me there."

I frown and nod, but before I can ask any more questions, he's gone, following the older man's path into the back.

"Shall we?" Ace asks, holding the front door open for me.

I look around the bar for a moment. Most everyone is back to focusing on whatever they were doing before Kolter and I appeared, but Star and Brick wave goodbye. Well, Brick puts his hand up and Star winks at me, but same thing.

"Sure," I say carefully then follow this motorcycle club member that I've never really met before, hoping Kolter is a decent judge of character and I don't end up sleeping with the fishes. Or is that a mob thing? I don't really know how all this gang stuff works quite yet.

Chapter Eighteen
Kolter

"What the fuck were you thinking?" Bones snarls the instant I shut the door behind me.

I don't answer. He doesn't actually want an excuse.

"Do you have any idea how incredibly stupid you were? Not only did you kill a civilian in the middle of a crowded club—our club—but instead of handling the mess yourself, you skipped away with that fucking girl and called in your buddies to clean things up?" he shouts, pacing back and forth beside the large meeting table.

"Leave her out of this," I say stiffly.

Bones' footsteps freeze in place, then he slowly turns to face me, head cocked to one side, his eyes narrowed. "What?"

"The girl. Leave her out of this. This is between you and me," I say, forcing a steadiness into my voice as I lift my chin.

Bones is the VP of our club, my dad's right-hand man. He's been running product and taking out enemies since before I was born. He lives and breathes for the club, which means when someone fucks up, like I just did, he'll burn down the fucking world to see them rectify what they've done. That's all fine—I've prepared myself; I've accepted it—but he won't speak ever about Naomi disrespectfully. In fact, I don't want her name or even a reference to her anywhere near his mouth.

His eyes rake over me for several moments, like he's trying to see something—or maybe hoping he doesn't see something? Either way, he looks pissed off.

Then he shakes his head. "You're fucking stupid."

No arguments there.

"Was it worth it? A fucking headache from hell, a body that needs to be properly disposed of and your father's fist down your throat, all for a quick lay?"

He's goading me, I know it, but as tempting as it is to react, I remain quiet—though my jaw clenches with such force my teeth might crack.

Bones shakes his head again as he looks down at his phone. "You know there's only so much we can keep from him, Kolt. If he finds out you killed some random over a woman?"

"She's not just any woman."

"Clearly—anyone with a pair of eyes can see the way you care about her. So, for the life of me, I can't understand why the fuck you thought it was a good idea to bring her here of all places? You could have taken her to your apartment, to her house, a fucking motel for Christ's sake. Here, though? Where damn near the entire fucking club has not only seen her but watched you with her?"

"It was a heat-of-the-moment thing," I reply, though it's a shitty defense. "I wasn't thinking clearly, could hardly fucking see straight. I knew I needed help with the clean-up, and I didn't know if she was gonna run to the cops after what she saw."

Bones lifts an eyebrow. "You killed the guy in front of her?"

I nod.

He scoffs. "How'd a suburban girl like her handle that?"

Oddly well. Took even me by surprise.

"I know who she is, Kolt," Bones sighs instead of waiting for my answer. His words are heavy, like it's a personal burden to know anything at all.

Bones' eyes come to mine then, a steady promise in them. "I don't know what you got in your head about that girl, but let me tell you one thing. If you care for her, you'll never speak to her again. If you don't, well, I still don't want to see her around here. We got enough damn problems, and I don't have time to deal with your pops shooting that poor girl dead in our bar."

His words chill me to the bone. Mainly because it's the truth. If my dad finds out about last night, he'll kick the shit out of me. If he finds out it was over a woman, a possible distraction, he'll kill her before I can even blink.

I should take Bones' advice. I should let her go, just like I did before. If I loved her the way I claim to, I would. I made a promise, though—to her, and I think to myself too. I'm not letting her go again, ever. I just have to be smarter from now on, and I will be. She's too important for me to make mistakes.

"Get the fuck out of here. Lie low before Snakes comes in. If he brings it up, I won't lie to him, but... I won't bring up the girl."

Sometimes, I wish Bones was my dad. He's been more of one to me than my own father ever has, and that right there, saying he'll go against the prez to protect me, or, more importantly, my girl... he's putting his life on the line for me, and I don't take that lightly.

"Thank you. And for what it's worth, I'm sorry. It won't happen again. I just... lost it."

Bones snorts, pulling a cigarette out of his pocket and lighting it up. "Yeah, well, you better fucking find it."

I nod my agreement, and he dismisses me with a simple wave, so I turn on my heel, make my way out the door and head down the hall. Several eyes move to me, curiously, as if I'm about to sit down and tell them everything we just discussed. Swear to fuck, these men are worse than a bunch of schoolgirls when it comes to gossip.

Fire Crotch attempts to leap into my arms, but when I don't

bother to catch her, she stumbles several steps then tries to recover with what's supposed to be a seductive smile.

"Where are you off to? I was thinking we could have a little fun this morning."

I don't even look at her, and I sure as fuck don't speak to her. Instead, I keep walking, pretending she's nothing more than a gnat in my way, though gnat is generous in this case.

Outside, I fire up my bike and take off down the road. First stop is my apartment for some fresh clothes and maybe a real shower. Then, despite Bones' warning, I'm off to where it really matters.

Chapter Nineteen
Naomi

Like he promised, Kolter came over for dinner. Well, it was more like lunch honestly, and that turned into dinner. We spent the whole day together. We watched movies with Mom; made meals. Mom and I even swindled him into a game of UNO, which he lost pathetically.

On the couch, I snuggled beneath a blanket, and Kolter's hand found its way beneath. He held my thigh the entire time, slowly teasing the apex of my legs. If Mom hadn't been there, I'd have jumped straight into his lap and... well, let's be honest, he would have talked me through it, but I wouldn't have minded. I swear, losing your virginity is something else. It's like once you finally experience what you've been missing all this time, suddenly you're addicted. Maybe that's just me, though, and it probably has everything to do with who I lost it to.

After Kolter left, Mom was on cloud nine. She smiled and sang while she did the dishes, talking about how good it felt to have her lost son back. I smiled too, agreeing, even if her calling Kolter her son had me feeling more than a little... ashamed? No, that's not right. I definitely have minimal shame for what Kolter and I share. Whatever it is, it's... different for sure. I mean, it's not every day you start dating your adopted brother after he kills the man who was going to take your virginity and takes it himself.

God. I should be much more disturbed by that sentence than I actually am.

Now I'm back in class, doing my best to focus on the professor's lecture.

Then my phone buzzes.

Kolter: Hey, Peaches. What are you doing tonight?

A smile touches my face, and I sense Cassi's eyes on me before she attempts to read the screen. I quickly tilt the phone away from her and tap out my reply.

Me: Just going to work on a paper. What's up?

Kolter: Work on it later. I'm taking you out. Be ready by seven.

Excitement fills me, and I have a hard time not bouncing in my seat as I text him back. Arianna and Cassi both notice my uptick in mood, and I can feel them staring at me like they're waiting for me to elaborate. It's too soon, though, right? I mean, they both have a lot on their plate, and... I don't want them to judge me. Especially Cassi. She'd have every right to, considering how I treated her, and that guilt is still eating away at me.

When the professor signals that class is over, everyone begins packing up, and I do the same—until I realize that Cassi and Arianna haven't moved. I lift my gaze from the desk to find them staring at me like they're waiting for something.

"What?" I ask.

Arianna smiles. "Oh, she's gonna play it like that, Cass."

"Like what?" I question.

"Like you didn't just spend the last few minutes giggling and squirming in your seat as you texted—" Cassi pauses, leaning over to look at my phone.

I quickly lock the screen, and she lifts an eyebrow as if to make her point.

"It's nothing," I say, but I can feel a deep flush settling into my cheeks.

"Bull-fucking-shit," Cassi retorts. "Come on, out with it."

I shake my head and stand, hoping I can just run away and they'll drop it. But who do I think I'm talking about here? My best friends chase after me, hot on my heels as they begin throwing out questions.

"Is it someone we know?"

"Is it someone we don't know?"

"Is it your mystery hookup from the club?"

"Just tell us something!"

"Yeah, you've been so distant for weeks now."

"Okay!" I snap, turning sharply on my heel to face them.

We're in the middle of the quad, other students rushing past us like a river around a boulder.

"I'm... seeing someone. It's new, and I'm not sure what will come of it, if anything, and I'm slightly nervous about being judged because you guys would have every right to, especially you," I say to Cassi.

"Why? You don't have a sister, so you can't steal her boyfriend," Cassi teases.

I rake my fingers through my hair. "It's complicated, and I... when I feel like I can tell you guys, I will. Is that okay?"

They both look at one another before Arianna gives me a soft nod.

"Of course it is, but, out of anyone, who are we to judge? I'm literally dating and living with my ex-stepdad."

"And I'm with my sister's ex-boyfriend," Cassi says.

I smile softly and nod, grateful for their acceptance. I want to tell them, I really do. Honestly, it would feel good for someone to know. To have someone tell me to keep my feet on the ground so I don't do something stupid like fall deeply and irrevocably in love with a dangerous forbidden man.

Too late for that, though.

———————

Seven feels like it takes forever to get here. I swear I've been staring at my phone for the last two hours, ready embarrassingly early. Mom asked me what I was doing getting all dressed up, so I admitted I had a date. When she tried to pry, I told her it was just some guy at school. I mean, what else was I supposed to tell her? Yeah, your adopted son is taking me out. Don't worry, family looks out for each other, I'll be safe. Yeah, absolutely not.

I told Kolter to text me when he was close so I could meet him on the corner, and as soon as my phone vibrates with that message, I'm flying out the door.

"Bye, Mom! Don't wait up!" I call out.

"He's not even gonna pick you up at the door? What a fucking schmuck," she calls as I shut the door behind me.

If she only knew.

I jog down the road until I reach the corner. And there's Kolter's bike pulled over to the side, the kickstand holding it up as he leans against it.

When he sees me, he pushes away from it and stalks towards me. Butterflies erupt inside me, so I pick up my pace.

When he holds his arms out, I leap into them without an ounce of hesitation; he catches me easily, pressing my body to his and cupping my butt.

I smile into his shoulder. "You copping a feel?"

"Fuck yes," he says like it's basic logic before pulling back so he can shoot me a grin.

He moves one hand to the back of my neck then and pulls me down for a kiss. It only lasts a few seconds, but it feels endless, the world around us fading away until it's just me and him under the evening sun.

He pulls back then presses another quick peck to my lips, like he couldn't help but steal one more taste before setting me down.

"Hope you're hungry, Peaches," he says, grabbing his helmet then strapping it onto my head.

"Is that a euphemism?" I tease.

His mouth lifts into a smile as he swats at my jeans. "Cute. Get on."

Kolter swings his leg over the saddle, and I slide behind him before he fires the bike up. Once my arms are wrapped around his waist, we take off down the road, and I rest the side of my head against his back, enjoying the warmth of him as the night air nips at me.

I don't even realize we've stopped until Kolter's hand taps my own, signaling that I should release him.

I quickly slide off the bike and look around. We're in the parking lot of an apartment complex. Couldn't tell you where, but the area looks nice.

Kolter helps me take the helmet off before slinging his arm round my shoulders and leading me to the front door. The man working the desk smiles and nods in greeting as we move towards the elevator. Kolter presses the number ten, and we arrive at our destination in a handful of heartbeats.

"So, I thought you were taking me out?" I ask as he leads us down the hall.

"You're not in your house, right? You're out," he tosses back.

I roll my eyes at him. "I was promised food."

He shakes his head as we stop in front of a door; he fishes out his keys and unlocks it. "I promised no such thing. I said 'hope you're hungry.'"

"A meal was implied," I scoff.

Kolter shrugs as he opens the door and holds it for me. "Your assumption from my conversation opener wasn't a confirmation of services or the receiving of goods."

I take a step into the apartment before narrowing my eyes at him. His stoic gaze is gone, replaced by a smart-alec smirk that lights up his stupid gorgeous face before he gives me a quick wink. Truthfully, I couldn't care less about food—I was just trying to give him a hard time; trying to be funny, I guess. He always thinks he has a leg up on me, though.

I continue into the apartment and hear the door shut behind me before Kolter follows me. It's a clean place—nice floors, crisp walls and furniture that looks like it's never even been touched, let alone used. It's not the type of place that screams someone lives here; more like a hideout of some sort, a getaway. But maybe it is. I haven't really asked him what his living arrangements are—maybe he spends most of his time at the clubhouse. I don't even know this is actually his place. Maybe it belongs to a friend.

"It's my place," Kolter says, as if he can read my thoughts.

I glance at him over my shoulder, and he raises an eyebrow.

"What? You act like I can't see every thought running through your head at all times."

I laugh. "Quite the superpower. Does it work on everyone?"

He doesn't laugh, though. He just closes the distance between us and rests his hands on my hips. "Only you."

Something in his voice kills my banter immediately, as well as any reasonable or witty response. I try to swallow, to clear the lump that's formed in my throat, and stare up at him.

"That's a pretty useless superpower. Only works on one person."

"Works on the only person who matters."

I smile softly and shake my head, giving him a light shove. "Please —there are plenty of people who matter."

Kolter slides a hand behind my neck, holding my gaze steady as he looks down at me. "Not to me."

"Kolt," I whisper roughly. "You're getting pretty intense for a first date."

"I don't intend to hide or minimize what I feel, Peaches. I told you I was all in; I meant it. You're just gonna have to deal with all that entails."

"Why does that sound like a threat?" I ask, tilting my head to one side.

"Because it should probably be taken as one."

It's stupid to smile, right? That wasn't romantic... was it? I mean, traditionally speaking, of course not. It gave more alpha-male, you're-my-property-and-I'm-a-bad-man vibes, but maybe that's why it's so romantic? Or maybe I've been listening to way too many of those dark romance audiobooks lately.

Kolter's hand drops to take hold of mine, then he leads me further into the apartment.

In the living room, there's a large TV accompanied by an entertainment center with a fireplace, a couch and a coffee table absolutely crammed with food. Any takeout food you could imagine, it's here—Mexican, Italian, sushi, Korean BBQ. There's even the iconic to-go box from my favorite pie restaurant in Seattle.

Yeah, you heard that right. A pie restaurant. It's literally everything.

"What is all this?" I ask as Kolter leads me to the couch.

"Food. You were whining about it the whole way up here," he says with a mock eyeroll.

I smack his shoulder and laugh. "You're a loser."

"Hey, you're the one that loves me," he says with a shrug.

A blush hits my cheeks at how casually he throws that out. That's dumb, right? I mean, we've had sex; we've exchanged the I love yous. This next part is only natural, right? Still, no matter how hard I try to school my expression, my smile grows, as does the flush coloring my face.

He notices too.

"I'll never get sick of you getting all rosy for me," he teases, wrapping his arm round my shoulder and pulling me into his side.

"You'd think you would—it's been happening practically our whole lives."

He brushes a lock of hair out of my face. "I loved it then too."

My heart flips as he stares into my eyes reverently, like he's attempting to commit them to memory, or maybe it's the moment he wants to save forever. Either way, same, because never in my life have things felt this... perfect.

"What are you having first?" Kolter asks, redirecting my attention towards the plethora of food.

"Well, I was going to go for the chips and queso until I saw the pie," I say, reaching out with grabby hands.

Kolter laughs and shakes his head. "How'd I know?"

He passes the pie box to me before taking some sushi for himself. I smile when I discover that it's a mud pie. Not the kind Mom used to make either—this is a peanut-butter-and-chocolate pie with chocolate fudge and whipped cream. It's a cavity waiting to happen, and I happily sink my teeth into a slice, humming my approval as I do a little happy bounce.

Kolter is watching me out the corner of his eye, a smile on his face, but I pretend not to notice as I grab the remote and turn on the TV. A football game flashes on, and Kolter reaches for the remote.

"Sorry, we can change it."

I pull the remote out of his reach and set it down. "I like football."

He furrows his brows and cocks his head to the side. "Since when?"

"Since Cassi screwed half the O line at our school," I say through a mouthful of pie.

Kolter lets out a surprised laugh, and I nod.

"As her designated wingwoman, I sat through a lot of games. The Seattle Crusaders are my favorite too," I say gesturing to the screen.

The camera pans just in time to catch Trevor Michaels, the team's quarterback, snapping the ball. He's one of the best quarterbacks in the league, and he knows it too. Aren't all pro players at least a little cocky, though? That's what makes them good, right?

Kolter and I spend the next few hours watching the game, eating until we can't move and just talking. We talk about my classes and my friends; we talk about Ace and everything Kolter's been up to these last few years. That conversation was pretty short. Lots of need-to-know information that I don't need to know, I guess.

Kolter checks his phone a few times, like he's waiting for a message—or maybe hoping one won't come through.

When he does it again, I finally ask, "Is everything okay?"

He pockets his phone. "Of course, Peaches. Why do you ask?"

I glance down at his pocket before giving him a flat look. "You've been checking your phone like you're waiting to win a radio contest. You trying to make sure your girlfriend stays out of the apartment?" I tease.

He scoffs and rolls his eyes. "My girl is sitting right next to me."

"So what is it then?"

"It's nothing," he says, shaking his head.

I continue staring at him, until he sighs and runs a hand through his hair.

"Just making sure I don't get called in for anything. I should be at the clubhouse tonight. Things have been... tense since the club."

I nod. "So why are you here then?"

"Because I promised I'd take you out. Because I wanted to see you. Because... I shouldn't be seen with you—or vice versa more like."

I frown. "Says who?"

"Bones."

"Is that the older guy from the clubhouse?"

Kolter nods.

"He doesn't like me?" I say with a joking smile.

"He doesn't like that I like you. It's dangerous, for you and me, especially if my dad finds out."

"So, what, we just have to sneak around until the end of time?" I ask, laughing.

When Kolter doesn't join in, though, my face falls.

"Oh."

He reaches out and squeezes my thigh. "Not forever; just for now. Besides, not sure Mom and your brothers are ready for us anyway."

"Will they ever be?"

"Fuck no. Nick is gonna be pissed. He always knew I had a thing for you."

"Really?" I ask, shocked.

"Yeah, why do you think he'd never let you hang out with us when I stayed the night before I moved in?"

"Because he's a jerk?"

He laughs. "True, but it's because he could tell that once you were in the room, all my attention went to you. Drove him crazy. We never talked about it directly, though. When Mom adopted me, I think he assumed it went away. I tried to make it."

"Me too," I admit.

So many nights I begged, prayed, manifested that the feelings I had for him would go away. When he legally became my brother, I felt wrong, dirty, but all that fighting was no use. On both sides, clearly.

"Wow," I breathe.

Kolter nods.

"And to think, we could have been hooking up for years."

An amused snort escapes Kolter, then he smiles. "Guess we better start making up for lost time."

Excitement surges through me as Kolter climbs on top of me and pins me to the couch.

"Be a good girl and scream for me, Peaches."

Chapter Twenty
Kolter

The last few weeks, I've spent every free moment I've had with Naomi. She's busy finishing up with classes, preparing for senior year and planning what she wants to do with her life after college. She's still set on being an investigative journalist, but in this day and age, that could really look like anything.

I won't lie: I'm more than against the summer internships she's been offered. Mainly because one is in San Francisco and the other is in Miami. Both are fucking far—away from home, away from Mom, away from me. I'd never stop her chasing her dreams but... fuck, if she sets her heart on it, I'm gonna have to figure something out because no fucking way is my girl moving down the coast or all the way across the fucking country. Even for a summer. It's not happening.

Most nights, she's been staying at my apartment. She's settled in quickly and has even suggested ways to warm the place up, make it feel more lived-in. I handed her a stack of cash from my safe and told her to go nuts. Whatever she wants to do, this place... it feels more like ours than mine.

With all the time I've been spending with Naomi, there's been little to none left for the club, hence why I'm in a meeting with my dad and Bones right now.

"The fuck is going on with you, huh? You're never at the club; I can never get you on your goddamn cell."

"I've been busy," I answer stiffly, regretting it instantly.

My father's eyes flash with danger, and his jaw tightens. "Alright, you've been busy. Doing what, exactly?"

I look down at the table beneath my clenched fist; I don't have an answer for him.

He reaches across in a flash, grabbing a fistful of my hair then smashing my face down into the table. Pain ricochets inside my skull, blood spurting from my nose as he releases his hold on me.

"Little fucking punk. When I ask you a goddamn question, you answer me. Now, what the fuck has got your head so far up your own ass that you aren't prioritizing the club?"

"I haven't missed church, or a drop. Does it matter if I don't spend every moment here?"

He smashes my face into the table again, and I blink blearily up at him as he leans over the table and glowers at me.

"Yeah, it fucking matters. You'll be staying at the club until further notice. Bones is gonna make sure of that. I'm heading over east for a few days, but when I get back, I think we'll assign you some more duties. Clearly, you don't have enough to do."

With that, my dad turns and heads out the door. Bones rises to his feet, giving me a disappointed headshake before following him out.

I sit in the meeting hall for another moment or two before pushing up from my seat and heading to the bathroom.

Once inside, I kick the door shut behind me then stare at myself in the mirror. Christ. I've definitely looked better, that's for sure.

I rummage around in the medicine cabinet, pull out a first aid kit and begin cleaning myself up. Some gauze, warm water and an ice pack later, I... still look like fucking hell. But I'm already running late for dinner.

When I step out of the bathroom, I run straight into Ace. He studies my face, his brows dipping in concern.

"The fuck happened to you?"

"Got in a fight with the table and lost," I scoff, pushing past him and making my way out of the clubhouse.

He follows right behind me, keeping his words to himself until we're outside, out of earshot.

"Where are you off to? Need some company?"

"Dinner," I answer shortly.

"With her?"

I don't respond; I just fire up my bike, but he moves closer, until his hands are resting on my bike and he's looking me straight in the eye.

"Look, man, I get it. I mean, she's beautiful and seems like a sweet girl."

"Careful," I grit through clenched teeth.

He lifts his hands in defense and shakes his head. "But you're playing a dangerous game. You keep giving your old man a reason to watch you close, and you're putting her directly in his path. I know you don't want that."

He's got a point, and it fucking irritates the shit out of me. What am I supposed to do, though? I can't be in two places at once, and if I have to choose where and how I spend my time, it's with her. Always. I've lost too much time with her already; I'm not willing to lose another second. Ace isn't wrong, though. My dad is suspicious, and my reaction in there didn't help.

Raking a hand through my hair, I let out an irritated sigh. "I hear you. I'll... I'll figure something out."

Ace watches me for a second, like he doesn't quite believe me, then nods. "Alright, man. Tell her I said hi."

I scoff at that, then back the bike up before taking off down the road. Life feels like a house of cards—one wrong move and everything will come tumbling down. Maybe it doesn't even require a wrong move, though. In this life, my life, it's simply inevitable.

Pushing the bike faster and faster, as if I can outrun any threat to us, I head for home, my real home. The one that's always been my safe space. I used to think that was because of Mom, because of our makeshift family, but now I know that comfort I felt, that safety, had way more to do with Naomi than even I understood. Because being with her... seeing her? It's like coming up for air after drowning. As if she only exists for my joy.

I turn into their quiet neighborhood and spot her in the front yard, pulling weeds from a flower bed. Slowing down, I pull into the driveway beside Nick's car. I didn't know he'd be here tonight.

It takes everything in me not to hold out my arms so Naomi can run to me. My fingers twitch and tingle, begging to feel her skin beneath them. But when she sees me, she jumps up and runs towards me anyway—before thinking better of it and slowing her steps. She looks around to ensure no one is watching then starts hurrying over to me once more.

I swing myself off my bike and pull her in for a hug. I release her faster than I want to and resist the desperate urge to taste her lips . Despite us waking up together and spending hours between the sheets this morning, it's never enough. She's more than just a drug— she's addiction embodied.

"Hi." She smiles shyly, tucking a piece of hair behind her ear.

"Hey, Peaches," I say with a barely there smile.

Her smile slowly falls as she studies me, concern stealing over her face. "What happened? Are you okay?"

I do my best to smile and wave away her worries. "I'm good."

The front door opens, and I hear Nick's loping footsteps before I see him.

"What's up fucker?" He grins as he closes the distance between us, pulling me in for a quick hug.

"Hey, man. I didn't know you were gonna make it."

"Me? What about you? Gone for six years and now you're coming over for regular dinners? That piece-of-shit dad kick rocks so you can actually live your life or what?"

"Nick," Naomi chastises.

Nick just rolls his eyes and playfully shoves her shoulder. "I'm teasing, kinda. Come on. Mom is making alfredo-stuffed shells," he says, biting his fist dramatically, like he can't wait to eat, though I'm pretty sure that's all the guy does.

I walk with him, glancing over my shoulder to watch Naomi gathering up her gardening tools before following us into the house. My feet pause as I debate turning round to help her then think better of it.

"Do I even want to know who fucked up your face?" Nick asks.

"Couldn't tell you if I wanted to," I say cryptically.

He nods like he understands. Even if it isn't necessarily a secret, no good comes from me talking about anything to do with the club. He gets that and, thankfully, he drops it.

The smell of garlic bread and pasta hits me as soon as I step through the door.

"Are all my boys here now?" Mom calls from the kitchen.

"I got the last one," Nick shouts triumphantly as we enter the kitchen and find Anthony helping dice something.

"Hey, brother," he says with a smile.

"Good to see you," I reply as Mom walks over and kisses me on the cheek.

"I'm glad you could make it, baby. Dinner is ready so grab a plate and dish up."

Anthony scrapes the vegetables on his cutting board into the salad bowl then heads over to wash his hands as Naomi steps into the kitchen.

Conversation comes easily, and we chat about our weeks—them more than me—as we dish up our plates. When we move to take our seats, I hang back for a moment to see where Naomi sits before casually dropping into the seat beside her. She gives me a small but knowing smile that has my heart tightening inside my chest. As much as I wish we didn't have to hide, I can't deny that sneaking around with her is the thrill of a fucking lifetime.

I scoot my chair all the way in so my legs are fully concealed, and Naomi does the same, so I'm able to easily rest my left hand on her inner thigh while we eat, and no one is any the wiser.

"So, I got tickets to next week's game. You in for some baseball and Seattle dogs?" Nick asks.

"The baseball part doesn't sound too bad. Hot dogs covered in cream cheese and grilled onions is where I draw the line," I reply, shaking my head.

Nick rolls his eyes. Our age-long debate of whether they're disgusting or delicious is alive and well, I see.

"Whatever, you can have your lame-ass mustard and relish while I have my delicious savory treat. You in?"

I laugh, but then my smile fades. My father's words ring in the back of my head, and suddenly my appetite is gone.

"Not sure I'll be able to get the time off. It's pretty busy right now."

Nick's disappointment is evident, but he nods. "No worries. I had a co-worker who was dying to go anyway."

"Or you could take me, your other brother?" Anthony interjects, easing the tension in the room.

Everyone chuckles—Anthony is the furthest thing from a sports fan.

"You're so whiney," Nick retorts before the conversation moves on.

After dinner, we all help clean the kitchen, but when we're done, I notice Naomi has disappeared. When I can't find her downstairs, I head up to her bedroom, knock gently on the door then push inside to find her sitting on her bed texting. She glances up at me and smiles before returning to her message.

"Hey, sorry. The group chat was blowing up."

"Everything okay?" I ask.

She nods. "Ari is engaged, and Cassi is moving across the country. A lot is changing."

I close the door behind me then sit down beside her on the bed. "Is change bad?"

Naomi shakes her head. "No, it's just... different." She laughs. "I mean, at the beginning of this year, I wouldn't have pictured any of our lives looking the way they do now."

I tilt my head to the side. "Yeah? What wouldn't you have seen for your life?" I ask, resting my hand on her thigh and caressing it with my thumb.

She smiles like she's making a point before her eyes move down to my hand.

"Um, this," she says, laughing. "I hadn't even seen you in years, and now you're... we're..." Naomi trails off, a deep blush settling into her cheeks.

"We're what, Peaches?" I ask, pressing a soft kiss to her neck.

She lets out a little huff but arches her neck to allow me better access. "Are you going to make me say it?"

"I'd like to hear it come from your mouth," I rumble against her skin then nip at the sensitive flesh.

She lets out another little huff, though it sounds more like a sigh. "Together. I hope, at least. I mean, we feel together to me."

I pause for a moment, pulling my face away so I can meet her eyes. They're full of lust but also a hint of hesitation—like she's not sure if what she said is going to push me away or not. My sweet, naïve girl. Does she not understand that hell itself couldn't keep us apart?

"We're more than together, Peaches."

A smile that lights up my goddamn soul spreads over her face. I reach out to cup her cheeks and press my lips to hers, unable to stop myself, and soon everything else fades away.

Slowly, I push her backward until she's lying on the bed then crawl on top of her. Our tongues twirl together as I swallow every moan that escapes her soft mouth. I begin to trace her curves with my hands, gripping the hem of her shirt and sliding it up—and then a hand wraps around the back of my neck, yanking me backward and throwing me to the ground.

The motion is jarring and unexpected, which means I don't see the fist driving into my face until it's too late. It's followed by a brutal kick to the stomach that knocks the wind out of my lungs and leaves me in a daze.

Naomi's scream shakes me free of it. I blink once and look up to see her on Nick's back, her arm wrapped around his throat as she attempts to drag him away from me.

Nick struggles for a moment before shoving her off him. She tumbles towards the bed but falls short, her back striking the edge of the bedframe before she falls to the ground. That has me instantly on my feet.

Nick tries to hit me once more, but I easily dodge him before driving my fist into his stomach. He coughs and wheezes, stumbling to the side as I rush to Naomi.

"Peaches, baby, are you okay?" I ask, my eyes roaming over her.

She arches her back slightly and winces before nodding.

"The fuck were you doing?"

Naomi smiles weakly. "I was trying to help. Thought I'd go all silverback on him."

I scoff and shake my head. She could have been seriously hurt. Her survival instincts are fucking abysmal. I'm gonna have to wrap her in bubble wrap and keep her in a bunker, I swear to God.

"What the hell is going on up here?" Anthony shouts as he barrels into the room, Mom right behind him.

"Ask him!" Nick sneers as he climbs to his feet.

Anthony and Mom look my way as I help Naomi to her feet.

"Well? Tell them!" Nick shouts. "Tell them what I just walked in on."

Before I even have a chance to respond, he continues. "He was on top of Naomi, forcing himself on her! You sick son of a bitch, she's my sister! She's *our* sister!" he snarls as Anthony steps between us.

Nick is rabid now, and Anthony lunges to hold him back. "I'll fucking kill you! You're dead, you hear me!"

"He did not force himself on me!" Naomi cuts in, trying to step in front of me, but I quickly wrap my hand around her waist and hold her in place. Nick is emotional and out of control right now. I don't know what he's capable of, and I won't risk her safety.

"Kolter and I are... together," she says, glancing at me before looking to the rest of our family. "We love each other; we have for a long time."

Anthony looks stunned; Nick looks like a raging bull and Mom just looks speechless.

"You grew up together! He groomed you! How can you not see that, Nay?" Nick spits, struggling against Anthony.

"Okay, that's enough!" Mom snaps. "Take him outside to cool down," she says to Anthony.

He begins hauling his brother away, but Nick doesn't stop fighting.

"You're dead to me! You fucking hear that! Sick psycho fuck!" he shouts, his protests growing fainter as Anthony drags him outside.

I squeeze Naomi's hip gently, and she turns to me, tears in her eyes, before burying her face into my chest. I hold her to me as she sobs.

Mom's gaze never leaves us. There's disappointment in her eyes, that's for sure, but also something else that I can't quite read. Understanding? Acceptance? Maybe I'm being a little too hopeful.

Chapter Twenty One
Naomi

After Anthony gets Nick to leave, I'm able to convince Kolter to go home, and my mom and I sit on my bed in silence for what feels like hours before she finally speaks.

"How long?"

I look up at her nervously, twisting my fingers together. "A little while."

"A little while as in weeks, months, years? I mean, were you together when he was living here?" she asks.

"No. I mean, I've definitely had feelings for him since then, but no. We didn't get together officially until a few weeks ago."

Mom nods to herself like that piece of information is a relief. She doesn't say anything more, though, which is extremely unlike her.

"You're mad, right?" I ask.

Stupid question, I know, but how else do I break this suffocating tension?

Her gaze meets mine, and her expression softens. "I'm... surprised, but no, baby. I'm not mad."

This catches me off guard.

Mom sighs and pats my leg. "Come on, Nay. We all know you've been in love with Kolter since before we adopted him. Nick and Anthony know it too, even if Nick doesn't want to admit it."

Yeah, to say the least.

"I always wondered if something would come of those feelings. If me bringing Kolter into the house would cause any issues. Between him and Nick, between you and Nick, between you and Kolter."

"They didn't."

"But they have now," she retorts with a heavy look. "I have a feeling Nick's reaction would have been similar whether Kolter was part of our family or not, though."

"He made Kolter sound gross, predatory. That's not what this is—it's not what we have," I say quietly, more to myself than anything.

My mom gives me a soft smile. "I know, sweetheart. I know your heart, and I know Kolter's. Which is why I know how beautifully you two fit. Our family dynamic makes things... unconventional to a stranger off the street, but since when do we care what others think?"

I'm truly stunned. I mean, this is not how I thought this conversation would go. Could anyone have seen this coming? Usually, when one of your brothers finds you making out with your other brother—granted we're not actually related—and your mom is there too... yeah, it doesn't usually end with a positive statement that you two are good together and who cares what anyone else thinks. My mom never ceases to amaze me.

"I love you, Nay, and I love Kolter too. I want the best for both of you, and if that's each other, then you'll always have my support."

Tears of relief prick my eyes, and I smile at her. "How did you become so amazing?"

She lets out a short laugh. "Single mom of three that turned into four. I learned quick to not sweat the small stuff."

I shake my head, my smile slipping. "I hate that he just left you, left us."

Mom's soft expression tightens, and she lifts a shoulder. "We all make our choices, and we all have to live with them. He missed out on some pretty amazing kids. That's his loss, not yours."

I nod, then my mom pulls me into a hug. I wrap my arms around her in return.

"I need you to promise me something, though," she says after a moment or two.

"Sure," I reply, pulling back to look at her.

"Whatever shit Kolter is caught up with. With the club and his dad and..." She sneers to herself, shaking her head before she rights her expression. "Promise me you'll stay far away from it, that he'll shield you from it. You'll always be my baby, and I know how nasty club life can be. That's one of the reasons I tried to get Kolter away from it when I did."

I choose not to explain how I know what she says is true. That will only send her into a panic. Besides, we're being careful.

"He's keeping me safe and away from... that stuff," I say cryptically.

Relief passes across my mom's face, and she presses a kiss to my temple.

"Good."

I called Kolter as soon as Mom left the room—he made me promise I would. He was just as surprised as I was when I told him how accepting she was, but reminded me that Nick wouldn't come around so easily. Obviously, I know that from his reaction, but it's still upsetting.

We stayed on the phone for another hour or so before he said he wanted to take me out to dinner the next day. I didn't want to question why he felt it was suddenly okay for us to be seen together. Maybe his hesitation was more about Nick than the club, and now that everything's all out in the open on that front, it's okay?

So now it's the next day, and I'm at Kolter's apartment getting ready for our date. Originally, I thought he was going to pick me up at my house, but he showed up in the morning with flowers for Mom and apologized for not telling her about us sooner. She made some threats, the way a mother should, about not hurting her little girl, he vehemently swore he never would and then we went on our way.

Kolter told me to dress nice, so I brought a little black dress I haven't worn yet, my favorite heels and my makeup bag. We spent most of the day just hanging out—when he wasn't devouring my pussy, that is.

I'm doing my makeup in the bathroom when my phone rings—it's the group chat FaceTiming me. I panic for a moment before I decide it wouldn't be a terrible thing to tell them the truth. They've called me out repeatedly now, and I've brushed them off every single time, but now my family knows, it's time, right?

I drop my makeup brush, accept the call and lift the phone up.

"Hey! Where are you?" Ari asks.

"Yeah, I'm in town finishing some stuff before I move and you're nowhere to be found! I want a girls' night!" Cassi adds.

"Oh, I'm sorry. I, um, have plans tonight. Can we do it tomorrow?"

Both girls look at me with suspicion.

"I mean, yes, but now we're extra curious. What are you doing tonight?" Cassi asks.

"I've been seeing someone," I admit.

Arianna laughs. "No shit—we know. You gonna finally reveal his identity or what?"

I open my mouth, struggling to find the best way to explain it—then Kolter strolls into the bathroom shirtless, cups my hip and presses a kiss to the side of my face.

"Sorry, baby. Just looking for—"

He pauses and looks down at the phone to see my two best

friends' jaws are on the floor. He glances at me before looking back to them.

"Hey, ladies. It's been a while."

"Kolter?" Arianna asks.

"You and Nay are... together?" Cassi says slowly.

His grip on me tightens, and a proud-looking smile spreads over his face. He presses another kiss to my cheek before turning to them again, as if that's all the explanation they need. Then he opens a drawer, grabs a comb and slips out of the bathroom like he didn't just drop an absolute bombshell.

Slowly, my eyes move back to the phone. My friends are so still I think the screen has frozen—until Cassi's ear-piercing shriek hits.

"OH MY GOD! OH MY GOD! OH MY GODDDD!"

"You and Kolter?" Arianna continues. "Wait, wait. Don't tell me..."

"Was he the guy you spent the night with at the club?" Cassi interjects.

I do my best to swallow down my nervous smile. "Yes."

"Oh, fuck!" Arianna exclaims, her eyes bright with excitement. "Wait, we never got any details, and now you have to tell us. Where did you run into him? How did this happen?"

Cassi is nodding hard, hanging on our every word.

I clear my throat. "Well, I found this hall, and it led to a bunch of rooms... with holes in the wall."

"A GLORY HOLE?" Cassi screeches. "You sucked your brother's cock through a glory hole and now you're together?"

"Jesus, Cass, he's adopted. He doesn't really count as her brother. Besides, she's been in love with him since she could, like, walk," Arianna retorts.

"I know! Still! No wonder you were being such a bitch to me—you had some guilt from your own naughty fun, didn't you?" Cassi teases, an understanding smile on her face.

"I still feel awful about how I acted about you and Nico," I admit.

Cassi waves me off. "Water under the bridge, babe. So, tell me, did you let your brother finally take your V-card?"

I mash my lips together and look down at the floor, sending both girls screeching once more.

"Holy fuck! Our baby is no longer a virgin!" Cassi grins. "I'm like a proud mama."

Arianna laughs. "You're such a fucking weirdo, Cass. Seriously, though, I mean, is me getting engaged to my ex-stepdad the least-taboo relationship in our group?"

Cassi and I both laugh.

"Does your mom know?" Cassi asks.

I grimace and nod. "And Nick, and Anthony."

"Oh shit, I do not like that reaction. Okay. Girls' night, tomorrow—we want every last detail. For now, go get railed by your brother! Love youuuu!" Cassi calls before hanging up.

I blow out a breath, then shake my head and laugh. I feel ridiculous for ever worrying about their reaction.

Kolter appears in the doorway wearing a dark button-up. "They're nosy," he says simply, leaning against the frame.

I scoff. "Were you eavesdropping?"

He shrugs. "Wasn't trying to. I'm pretty sure you could hear Cassi from Canada, though."

A laugh escapes me as I tug my lipstick out my bag.

But Kolter grabs my hand and holds it in place, looking down at me. "You okay, Peaches?"

"Honestly, yeah. I know things are still a mess with Nick and probably will be for a while, but now that Mom knows, and Anthony and my friends... it makes us feel... real. Does that make any sense?"

He stares down at me, his eyes glimmering as he nods once. Then his lips ghost over mine gently, and when he pulls away, he rests his forehead against my own.

"I love you, so fucking much."

"I love you too," I whisper roughly.

Slowly, he pulls back, releasing my hand—but not before plucking the lipstick from my grasp.

"Hey, I need that," I cry. But then one of his hands is grabbing the side of my mouth while the other pops the cap off the lipstick.

I freeze as he slowly drags the stick against my lips, delicately painting the top and then the bottom. It's almost hypnotic the way he looks—so focused, so intense. When he's finished, he sets the tube down and stares at me in admiration.

"How do I look?" I ask softly.

Kolter doesn't reply. Instead, he drags my lips to his, nipping, sucking and all but consuming them before pulling away roughly. I'm left breathless as he reaches up and drags his thumb against the corner of my mouth, smearing the lipstick further.

"You look like mine."

Without another word, we come crashing together. I leap into his arms, and he holds me to him tightly. Our tongues tangle around one another as I sink my teeth into his lip. He groans at the slight pain before returning the gesture in kind.

I feel us moving but am too busy to care where he's taking us.

When we reach the bedroom, he sits us down on the edge of the bed so I'm perched in his lap. Then he's dragging the hem of my dress up and pulling my panties to the side. The head of his cock presses against me, and I spread my legs further so that I can lower myself onto him.

It doesn't matter how many times we do it, it still hurts at first, and I wince as I slide down, inch by inch, savoring his moans.

"Goddamnit," he grits through clenched teeth.

I attempt to control my breathing, but it sounds more like panting, so I pull away from him for a minute, closing my eyes as I force myself down until I'm fully seated on him.

"Peaches, look at me," he says, demanding and desperate.

I blink my eyes open and find him already staring at me with the kind of reverence you'd expect from a worshipper to a deity. His gaze traces over my face, and he shakes his head like he's in awe before his hands settle on my hips.

"You're perfect."

I smile softly, lifting my hips and causing him to groan once again.

"You are," I whisper, lifting them again, and again, slowly finding a rhythm.

He laughs. "Fuck no. But for you, I'll always try to be."

My heart melts as his words as our bodies push together. A moan escapes me, and the tension I felt before begins to ease, each thrust more and more comfortable.

"That alright, Peaches?" he asks, his breath choppy.

"Mhmm," I reply before letting out another moan .

"Good, now be my sweet girl and fucking ride me."

Excitement surges through me as I pick up the pace of my thrusts. I don't have a lot of experience being on top. Usually, we're in such a rush, filled with passion and lust, that we don't take a moment to do anything but be with each other as fast as humanely possible. That's always amazing, don't get me wrong, but this? I feel in control, powerful, and having a man like Kolter looking up at me in wonder spurs on my every move.

Kolter moves his hand to my clit, rubbing quick, tight circles against it with two fingers.

"More," I beg.

He does as I ask, his hips meeting mine thrust for thrust, pushing him deeper inside me.

"Oh my gosh, y-yes, just like that," I stammer.

"Take what you want, baby—I'm all yours."

My toes curl in the sheets, and my thighs burn, begging me to stop. Nothing will take me away from this moment, though. Especially not when I feel Kolter's body tense beneath me, his hips lifting and his cock pulsing inside me. A few more quick rubs to my clit and

I'm shattering apart, following right alongside him, our groans of pleasure shaking the walls.

Finally, I collapse against his chest, and for a while, we just lie there in a daze, our breathing still heavy. I can't imagine how life could get any better. It's perfect; it's beyond my wildest dreams.

He runs a hand through my hair then, gently demanding my attention. I look up at him and smile, only to find him doing the same. He traces the outline of my lips with his thumb, cleaning up the smeared lipstick before he says, "I think you should start wearing it like this more often."

Chapter Twenty Two
Kolter

I keep my hand on Naomi's lower back as we step into the restaurant. The gentle sound of smooth jazz plays all around us; there are low, soft-lit chandeliers decorating every inch of the ceiling; and waiters in crisp black-and-white uniforms glide back and forth, offering the finest bottles of wine and trays of delicacies.

It's not my vibe at all.

But the way Naomi's eyes light up when she takes in her surroundings makes it all worth it. She's never been the type to value money or status, but we didn't exactly grow up with it either. Over the years, through legal means and otherwise, I've grown incredibly wealthy, and while I've treated myself to bikes, a nice apartment and other basic luxuries, Naomi hasn't experienced any of that. And I want to give her everything this life has to offer. Everything *I* can possibly offer her.

I know that will never be enough, given what she truly deserves, but I'll fight like hell every day to make myself worthy of her.

"Good evening. Reservation?" the hostess asks.

I nod. "Under Jacobson."

Naomi gives me an odd look, but the hostess just smiles.

"Right this way."

"Since when is your last name Jacobson?" Naomi whispers over her shoulder to me as the hostess guides us through the restaurant.

"They don't need a real name, and it's better this way," I respond, pulling out her chair for her then scooting it in while the hostess places the menus on the table.

"Why?" she asks as I take my seat.

"Why what?"

"Why is it better to use a fake name?"

I look at her for a moment, the answer on the tip of my tongue before I think better of it. Instead, I grab the menu off the table and start browsing through it. I can feel her gaze on me like a laser, but I don't give in.

"Your life is really dangerous, huh?" she says, almost to herself. "Like, there are people out there who want to hurt you—who might want to hurt me?"

I set the menu down and find her watching me with a deep frown. Her tone isn't concerned, though, just accepting—as if she already knew all of this to be true but is just now confirming it. I don't like to sugar-coat things, and she's too smart for me to even attempt to lie to. I'll withhold certain information, but this is hardly a secret.

"Yes."

She nods, picking up her own menu and disappearing behind it. "Kinda wish you'd lied."

A dry laugh escapes me as I pull her menu down so I can look her in the eye. Her expression is sad, heavy, but still accepting.

I take her hand in mine and graze my thumb over the back of it. Fuck. Her skin is like silk. There isn't an inch of her that isn't perfection.

"You never have to worry, okay? I will always keep you safe—never doubt that."

She gives me a sad smile. "I know. It's you I'm worried about. As important as I am to you, that's what you are to me. You get that, right?"

I blink slowly. I've never considered that before. Mainly because I don't see how it's possible for anyone, even Naomi, to love someone as much as I love her. The anguish hiding just beneath the surface gives her away, though, so I nod and deliver her a new promise.

"I will always come home to you—always."

Hope flickers in her eyes, and it's exactly what I was craving. I know it's a promise I shouldn't have made. It's definitely one that I can't keep, but if it gives her even an ounce of relief, then it was all worth it.

We start with a few appetizers and a bottle of red before ordering our entrees. Naomi fills the conversation with so many topics, it's almost difficult to follow. I don't mind, though—I'd happily sit here for hours, listening to her bounce from topic to topic with her hand in mine.

She looks past me then as if the waiter is approaching, but her smile fades, and I turn to see it's not the waiter standing there—it's my father.

"Isn't this a lovely sight?" He smiles, all teeth.

Bones is standing behind him, stoic and stiff as always. The two of them are in their leathers, their appearance a stark contrast to the restaurant's patrons, and they all notice too. Several tables turn their attention to us, soft whispers filling the air.

I do my best to stay calm and unfazed on the surface, but on the inside, I'm flipping the fuck out. How did he find me? I intentionally took us over an hour away, somewhere I was certain no one would stumble across us. The only way he could know is if he followed us, which means he's been watching me far closer than I realized.

"They have the best steak around supposedly," I answer coolly.

"That so? We may just have to pull up a chair and join you," he says to Bones before turning his attention to Naomi.

"Well, don't be rude, boy. Introduce me to your date."

The way he says *date* sends something slithering down my spine, but I do my best to keep my tone unaffected as I slowly remove my hold on Naomi's hand and gesture to her.

"This is Naomi. Naomi, this is my father Matthew."

A light flickers in my father's eyes as Naomi holds out her hand to shake his.

"It's nice to officially meet you," she says, ever polite, but I hear the reservation in her voice.

She's never crossed paths with my father—I've never allowed it to happen. She's heard plenty about him, though.

"Amy's daughter? I'll be damned—you're the spitting image of her," my dad exclaims, smiling down at Naomi and holding her hand far longer than I care for.

Naomi swallows nervously, carefully extracting her hand from his grip as she gives him a tense smile.

"Well, I can only assume this is what you've been so busy with. Can't say I blame you, son. What a looker," my father says as his eyes rake over Naomi.

My hand twitches, just begging to reach for the knife concealed in my pocket. Fantasies of jamming that knife right through his eye socket so he can never look at her dance in my head. It takes nearly everything in me to sit there silently instead.

My father's eyes narrow on me—he's clearly irritated by my lack of reaction. "You should bring her by the club some time. We can have dinner. Properly get to know one another. If you plan on making her your old lady, we have rules now, don't we?" he goads.

"Sure, sometime," I agree.

"Tomorrow," he counters, a wicked gleam in his eye.

"Can't," I counter.

"I insist," he hisses, the look in his eye promising that I don't want to push this matter further.

Begrudgingly, I respond with a terse nod, and he claps my shoulder roughly.

"Good. See you both there. Enjoy your meal."

And he turns and walks out of the restaurant.

Bones shakes his head at us and sneers before following him out.

I don't realize how long I stare after them, making sure they've actually left, until Naomi tentatively rests her hand on mine.

"Kolter, are you okay?"

Words escape me as I try to pull myself together. No. I'm not fucking okay. She has no idea how out of control things have become. How those promises I made only an hour ago are already burning to a crisp, disintegrating faster than it took me to utter them.

But I push that all down and force a smile onto my face.

"Everything is fine, Peaches."

Chapter Twenty Three
Naomi

We moved our girls' night to a girls' day because of the dinner tonight. Ari and Cassi didn't mind at all, and it was really nice to finally talk to them about everything that's been going on. I mean, I kept some of the details vague—I know better than to disclose the whole murder part of how Kolter and I got together. I'm honestly impressed how casual I feel about the whole thing, though I'm pretty sure that makes me a horrible person.

The man was mentioned on the news the other day actually—an appeal for any information about his whereabouts, with a sobbing woman and a little girl in the background. My stomach soured at that, but as sad as I am for that little girl losing her father, I felt less guilty that the piece of shit who was cheating on his wife got his come-uppance.

Now that my girls' day is over, I'm on my way to the clubhouse. Kolter texted me the address since I had no idea where to go. I was a little pre-occupied last time I was there.

I'll be honest, I expected Kolter to pick me up and drive me. He usually doesn't like me driving, even though I constantly remind him that we're way more likely to be in an accident on his bike than I am in my car. Still, he usually insists. Not tonight, though. He said he wanted me to have an easy way to get home. Which I took to mean, *In case I need you to get out of there without me.*

Maybe I'm expecting this to be way more than it is. I mean, I've been there before. It's just dinner—it's not like there's going to be a shootout or anything. I think. To be honest, I may or may not have been reading some MC romance books, and I think I've put myself on edge.

When I pull up to the club, there are men of varying sizes and ages sitting outside, and all of them turn the same unwelcoming narrow-eyed glare my way.

Swallowing roughly, I gather all my nerves, push the door open and step out of the car, but instantly feel uncomfortable. Kolter told me to dress casual, that it didn't matter what I wore, but it's like he doesn't understand women at all?

Finally, I settled on a pair of light-wash blue jeans and a white lace blouse with white sandals. The sun is out today, which is a rarity for Seattle, and I thought the outfit was appropriate for the nice weather. But given how the bikers are all staring at me like I'm a zoo animal, it's clear I was wrong.

Keeping my head held high, I make for the front stairs, but a large body steps in front of me, blocking my way. I pause for a moment then attempt to sidestep him. He matches the move, smirking down at me as he pushes his gut against my chest.

"Excuse me," I say softly, making sure I don't make eye contact.

"You're excused. What's a sweet little thing like you doing at a place like this? You lost?"

I don't respond, attempting to step past him once more, but of course he blocks my path again. His hand wraps around my bicep and squeezes, and his teasing tone turns menacing.

"You little bitch, I'm talking to you. What are you doing here?" he snarls.

A large hand covered in tattoos claps down on the man's shoulder, forcing him to look up to see who's dared to interrupt his fun.

It's Bones. Kolter said he was the VP of the club, his dad's right-hand man.

Bones stares down at the other biker, tightening his grip on his shoulder. "Let her go."

The man releases me quickly, lifting his hands up in a show of innocence. "Sorry, didn't know she was yours. Little younger than you normally go for, eh?"

Bones' head cracks forward, and there's a sickening crunch as it connects with the other man's nose. He crumples, holding his face as he moans and writhes on the ground.

Bones looks to me.

"Thanks," I say softly.

But his expression turns to one of disgust before he shakes his head and turns to go back inside.

I shoot one more glance at the man on the ground, then make my way up the stairs and into the clubhouse.

When I step inside, I notice the place looks a little different from last time. Several tables have been rearranged to form one long banquet table with chairs all around it. I recognize a few faces, like Ace and Brick, who both nod in greeting before Kolter steps out from the back. His eyes land on me instantly, and he closes the distance between us as he takes a visual inventory.

"Are you hurt?" he asks with a deep frown.

"No, of course not."

His gaze pauses on my bicep, and I look down to see the skin is a little red there. No big deal, right? You wouldn't think that if you saw Kolter's reaction—his eyes go black, and his face turns white with rage.

Kolter moves to take a step around me, but then Bones and Matthew emerge from the back.

Matthew calls out a single word: "Sit."

Kolter tenses, freezing in place, then turns to the two chairs before us. He pulls out one for me then slides into the seat beside me. I don't miss how he puts himself between his father and me, a gesture I'm more than grateful for.

Matthew watches us with a curious grin that exposes his yellowing teeth as he lights a cigarette. "Who the fuck is this gentleman? Anyone recognize him?" he teases, looking around the quickly filling table.

Several guys come in from out front, the man from earlier along with them. His eyes find me instantly, and his gaze narrows with contempt. Across the table, Ace stands up, grabbing his bottle of beer then making his way round the table to take the empty seat beside me.

When he sits down, he gives me a quick nod and a barely there grin before shooting a glare at the man. One I bet doesn't even rival the one Kolter is no doubt giving him over my shoulder.

"Dough Boy, if you think you're gonna sit at my table and bleed all over it, you got another thing coming. Go fucking clean yourself up," Matthew snarls.

The man glares at Bones before softening his expression and nodding at Matthew, the way any submissive dog would yield to an alpha.

"Dough Boy?" I ask Kolter as softly as I can.

Not softly enough, though, because Matthew responds, "Yeah, because he's a fat piece of shit with nothing else to offer."

The man doesn't turn round, doesn't act like he hears Matthew at all. He just keeps walking to what I assume is a bathroom, shutting the door behind him with a rough slam.

Matthew shakes his head at me. "Sorry about the welcome. Afraid my boys aren't too used to pretty little things wandering in here."

"Yeah, the old hags are the ones who usually hang around," Ace throws out, causing laughter to rumble round the room.

I know he jumped into the conversation to steer it away from me, and though I appreciate it, it doesn't work.

"So, Naomi, can I interest you in an appetizer?" Matthew asks, holding up a small bag of white powder.

I frown as Kolter's hand slides to my thigh, gripping it tightly.

"She doesn't touch that shit," he answers for me.

"Just because she hasn't tried it doesn't mean she doesn't want to," Matthew says to his son before turning back to me.

I quickly shake my head before thinking to add, "Thank you, though, for the offer."

Matthew stares at me for several seconds before tilting his head to one side. "You sure you're Amy's girl? She never turned down shit back in the day. Was practically a fiend for it."

I don't believe a word he says. My mom? Doing drugs? Highly unlikely. This is the woman that literally beat Anthony's ass with a wooden spoon when she found a baggie of weed in his sock drawer when he was sixteen.

I know Mom grew up with Matthew, but though she's never gone into detail, it always sounded like they didn't run in the same social circles, so I can't imagine he knows what he's talking about.

"She doesn't fucking touch the stuff," Kolter repeats.

Matthew shoots Kolter a threatening look and sticks a finger in his face. "Better watch how you fucking speak to me in front of company, boy."

Kolter's body goes rigid, and the tension between the two of them is enough to choke every last one of us. It eases a moment later when Dough Boy comes out of the bathroom, taking the furthest seat from Kolter and I before another guy comes out the back carrying a big pot of what smells like chili, followed by a plate piled so high with cornbread, I can't even tell what color the plate is.

Everyone begins tearing into the food like animals—like they haven't eaten in days. Kolter dishes me up a bowl before serving himself, and I take a few bites until something in it sours my tastebuds.

Matthew watches me closely before his eyes narrow. "Is something wrong? You don't like Frenchie's cooking?"

"No, it's great. I'm just not very hungry."

Matthew watches me for several more moments then shakes his head and busies himself with his meal.

The other men finish, taking their bowls to the back then filing out of the place one by one, until it's just Bones, Matthew, Kolter, Ace and me left.

"So, Blade says you're in school?" Matthew asks.

It takes me a moment to remember Kolter's club name, and I nod.

"Smart girl. Bet you get real good grades too."

"I do my best."

"I'll bet you do. Probably get your brains from that button-up pansy of a father. What's he up to these days?" Matthew asks as he pours himself a glass of whisky.

"I don't know. He left when I was a baby," I say with a shrug.

Matthew cocks his head to the side and looks at Bones. "I didn't know that. Did you?"

Bones nods.

"Amy always knew how to drive them away. She sure was worth the trouble, though." Matthew grins, visibly adjusting himself through his trousers.

My stomach turns, and I look away so I don't puke up the little bit of vile chili in my system.

"Oh come on," he coaxes. "You can't be that uptight—I know my boy here can be rough with the women he fucks. We're all family here. No need to be shy."

Kolter's face is stoic. He doesn't look towards his dad or to me; he just stares forward.

I clear my throat. "I'm not shy."

"You're not?" Matthew flashes me a bullshit smile.

I shake my head, driving my point home. "I just don't enjoy discussing whether my mother is a good lay or my boyfriend fucking anyone but me."

The words slip off my tongue, surprising even me. I certainly surprise Kolter. I never swear, and I definitely never speak so... directly. And now of all times, this is the moment I decide to do so? Awesome, Nay.

Matthew is quiet for a moment—then he slams his fist down on the table and bellows with laughter.

"Oh shit. You've got a little bit of fire in you, don't ya? I didn't expect that. That's good. You'll stick around longer that way."

"You mean around the club?" I ask.

"I mean in life," he throws back, turning my stomach instantly.

He gives me a smile that feels equal parts menacing and amused then rises from the table.

"Well, business calls. Thanks for coming by. You should bring her more often, Blade," he says, making his way towards the front door.

But he pauses just behind me, his hand sliding to the front of my neck, barely gripping it but still keeping it firmly in place as his breath fans over my cheek.

"Oh, and if you ever get in the way of Blade's responsibilities to the club again, I'll snap your goddamn neck."

My pulse thunders, and my eyes widen in shock—then he releases his hold on me and swaggers out of the club like he owns the whole damn world.

The rest of the table is frozen in place, my heavy breathing the only sound, then Bones pushes up from his seat.

"Get her out of here," he rasps before heading out the door after Matthew.

"What was that about?" I ask almost numbly, glancing to Ace then Kolter.

Kolter's eyes meet mine, a heavy level of... something behind them.

"It was a warning."

"To me?" I ask.

"To me," he clarifies.

He glances at Ace, who nods wordlessly and heads for the door, then Kolter stands and takes my hand, pulling me to my feet.

"Where are we going?" I ask.

"You're going home. Ace is gonna follow you to make sure you get there safe."

I frown. "What about you?"

He runs a hand through his hair and lets out a rough sigh. "I gotta go handle some shit."

Chapter Twenty Four
Kolter

Since I was forced to bring Naomi to the club for dinner, my father has done everything in his power to keep me as busy as possible. Part of it could be because I've all but shrugged off every responsibility he's tasked me with until now, but I know the truth. He wants to keep me busy, away from her, drown me in duties until I can't see anything but the club.

I pull out my phone and send Naomi a goodnight text. It's 2:30 a.m, and I know she'll have been out for hours. Still, it'll make her feel better when she reads it in the morning. I'll also send her a good-morning text before I finally crash. I want her to know that even when I can't be with her, I'm thinking of her. Always.

The salty stench of the port fills my nose, and I wrap my jacket tighter around me as the crisp night air bites through my clothes. For the last two weeks, I've been making drops, collecting debts and doing every grunt job possible. Tonight, though, Snakes had something else in mind. He said I'd been doing good work and sent me with a small group of guys to pick up a shipment. Apparently, the Delfino family, the local mafia, have been sniffing around our territory and are planning to cause some shit tonight.

I'm surprised he and Bones didn't want to be here. They don't usually turn down a good fight, and they definitely never turn down an opportunity to take out a few mafia brats. As usual, though, I'm not allowed to question plans or motives; instead, I do as I'm told, I get out, and I hope I live long enough to see one more smile from my Peaches.

Leaning against the wall, I absentmindedly mess with my knife, flicking it out and in, over and over again, as I study the shoreline. Ace watches me with amusement before bumping his shoulder into mine.

"You good?"

"I'm fine," I respond, standing up a little straighter.

He laughs. "Bullshit. You're a million miles away. Or thirteen to be exact," he says with a wink.

I blow out a breath and look up at the sky. Thirteen miles—is that it? That's the distance between me and my girl? Feels like a lot more.

"How much are we picking up? Are two vans gonna cut it?" Ace asks, looking at the two cargo vans idling to one side.

I pull out a cigarette, light it and take a drag before shaking my head. "You think he tells me shit? He said go pick up the shipment at this place, this time and if any mafia fucks come by, gun 'em down."

"Aye aye, captain," Ace mocks.

I scoff in agreement and take another drag then spot a boat beginning to pull into port. It's unmarked, too small to be commercial and looks to be our supplier.

I smack Ace's chest then gesture to the boat before looking round at the dozen guys I brought with me. Several stay with the vans; the rest follow me to the dock.

Once the boat is anchored, we're led wordlessly on board, then to a cargo area filled with dozens of wooden crates. I signal to Bunky, who hands over his crowbar, then crack open one of the crates to reveal a fuck ton of AK-47s and AR-15s, and several thousand rounds of ammo for each. I nod in approval, then start organizing the offloading, which is going to take a few journeys each.

We're almost done when Ace—who I've been carrying crates with—stops walking and turns his head slowly to the side.

"Those headlights, Blade?"

I follow his gaze and spot several vehicles approaching our position.

"Son of a bitch," I mutter, then turn to the rest of my guys and shout, "Fucking hurry! We got company!"

Some of the guys rush back to the boat to finish offloading the cargo; the rest of us grab our guns and tuck ourselves behind the vans and the building. The cars come to a slow halt, and for a moment, I think they haven't seen us—until the shots ring out.

The last crate is being carried across the parking lot, and it makes for a perfect fucking target. It's quickly riddled with bullet holes, and then one of my guys gets hit. He drops to the ground, the crate falling along with him, but his buddy grabs him by the vest and pulls him out of the way. From there, it's a full-on war.

Men rush from our left and right, shooting from a distance before getting close enough that it becomes a hand-to-hand fight. I smack a gun out of one mafia prick's hand, headbutting him for good measure before jamming the butt of my own gun into the back of his head. The next man that comes at me, I sink my knife into his gut, ripping upwards with a sharp yank that drops him to the ground.

The shipyard is littered with bodies. Some are my men; some are theirs. It's a goddamn ambush, a bloodbath, and all any of us can do in the moment is fight like hell to make it out the other side.

I rip one guy off Bunky, driving my knife into his forehead before ripping it back out, then look around to see who to take on next

A bullet whizzes by my head, and I whip round, diving out of the way before the next shot comes.

It's Luis Delfino, a prince of sorts within their family and the most arrogant piece of shit you've ever met.

When his clip runs empty, I charge towards him. The mafia love their guns, and don't get me wrong, so do we, but they're prissy and don't enjoy a good street fight. Not like I do, at least.

I tackle him to the ground—both of us landing heavily on the concrete—then drive my fist into his face. His head whips back, and he spits blood at me before kneeing me in the balls.

Bitch fucking move.

I roll onto my side, attempting to catch my breath, but he delivers a swift kick to my stomach that causes something inside me to pop.

"You inbred Neanderthals really thought you could steal my shipment?" he sneers, delivering another brutal kick to my stomach. "Thought I wouldn't stop you? I believed you to be smarter than you looked, but I suppose that was foolish of me."

He goes to kick me again, but I slice the back of his ankle with my knife, severing his Achilles tendon. He cries out and drops like a stone.

I pin him to the ground and press my gun to his temple. "The fuck are you talking about? This is our shipment. You're trying to rob us," I sneer into his face.

He looks at me like I'm stupid, still wincing in pain. "Of course you don't even know who owns the product you're taking. All you do is take orders like a good little bitch."

Anger surges through me, but when I pull the trigger, the clip ticks. I try again and again, but I'm out of bullets.

That hesitation is all the opening he needs to deliver a punch to my face and wiggle out from under me. He starts crawling towards a gun lying beside one of his fallen men, and I decide we need to get the fuck out of here.

I jump to my feet then run to the van, limping slightly. Several of my guys, Ace included, are already there.

"Let's go!" I shout, and we all pile into the vans as soon as we have an opening.

I try to work out who made it as both vans peel out of the parking lot. Several shots fire after us, shattering the windows before we turn the corner.

"What the fuck!" I shout, kicking one of the crates in the back.

"Easy, Blade. We got the supply. That's what matters," Ace wheezes, drawing my attention.

His face is bloodied all to hell and he's holding his side.

"You good?" I ask him.

He winces and nods. "Shallow entry wound. Still, probably gonna need the doc."

"That makes all of us," Bunky scoffs as he whips the wheel round.

"How many are in the other van?" I ask, since it's only me, Ace and Bunky in here.

"Three," Bunky answers gruffly.

"Jesus," Ace mutters.

We came with ten. That means four of our guys are either dead or about to be. Over what? Some fucking stolen product?

When we pull into the drop spot, I'm fucking livid. I fly out of the van and storm towards my father and Bones; they both look bored, impatient, like they've been waiting on us all goddamn night.

I don't think—I just act, driving my fist into my father's face. His head snaps to one side in a way that's deeply satisfying.

Bones is quick to pull me off him, and to my surprise, my father doesn't react. At least not the way I expected. Instead, he smiles at me, like he's impressed.

"What the hell was that?" I snarl.

"Did you get the shipment?" he asks.

I let out a bitter laugh, struggling against Bones. "You mean the stolen weapons? The ones that belong to the Delfino family? Yeah, we fucking got 'em. And four of our guys are six feet under for it!"

My father frowns. "Four? Jesus, were you guys fucking around? I told you that you'd have company. You weren't better prepared?"

My eyes practically bug out of my head. "You told us they might try to poach our shit. Not that they'd be coming to collect theirs! Every one of those men's lives is on your head!"

He gives me a doubtful look. "Be pissed all you want, but you were the man in charge out there. So every life lost is on you," he says, pointing his cigarette at me.

"Now get the fuck outta my face," he continues. "Take your bitch ass home."

I look to Bones, surprised to see a pinched expression on his face. He always knows what my father is up to, yet he looks just as blind-sided as I feel. Of course, he doesn't speak, but his concern is heavy in his eyes, which unnerves me. We've never provoked the mafia like this, just as they've never provoked us. We have our fights, our territorial disputes, but we know an intentional war is a death sentence for all.

I guess Snakes doesn't give a shit, though.

Chapter Twenty Five
Naomi

It's been nearly three weeks since I went to the club with Kolter. Since then, he's been avoiding me—or that's the way it feels anyway. Last night was the first time he picked me up, took me out then brought me back to his place. I was starting to feel like he didn't want to be with me or something. Which I know sounds ridiculous and insecure since we literally text all day long. It's not the same, though. Something feels different, and I have this gut feeling it has everything to do with his dad.

I haven't been able to shake the things he said about my mom. Every syllable Matthew utters feels intentional, strategic. I'm just trying to figure out what he has to gain by giving those pieces away, even if I think they're bullshit. I've wanted to bring it up to my mom, but we've talked about Kolter's dad a lot throughout the years. She and my dad went to school with him—he was always in trouble, always looking for a fight and was never good news. And that's where I thought it ended. Something about Matthew's version makes me feel like there's more to it, though.

Kolter had to go do something for the club this morning, and I need to get all these thoughts out of my head, so I'm heading home to talk with her.

Another person pops into my head. Nick. I haven't heard from him since he blew up at dinner. It's not like we're the type of siblings to stay in contact all day, every day, but it's been a while, and this radio silence needs to end.

I glance back and forth between the road and my phone before I hit call on Nick's contact. The phone rings through my car speakers once, twice, three times.

"Seriously, you're going to be that big of a child about all this?" I mutter, not realizing the call has connected until he says, "That really how you want to start this conversation?"

I straighten up in my seat like he can see me and shake my head. "Sorry. I didn't think you were going to answer."

"So you settled for talking shit behind my back?" he scoffs.

"No, I just..." I pause and take a deep breath. "I'm sorry. I'm sorry that Kolter and I being together upsets you. I'm sorry that it surprises you, and I'm sorry that you had to find out that way. I'm not going to apologize for the love we share or our relationship, though."

I can practically see his sneer, along with his brisk pacing, given the uptick in his breathing.

"Relationship? Naomi, get a fucking grip. He's using you. He groomed you to worship the ground he walked on, and when he's finished, he'll toss you to the side just like every woman that came before you."

I'm stunned into silence at the anger in his words, then I shake my head again.

"You're wrong."

"Or maybe you're gullible," he throws back.

I let out a heavy exhale as I come to a red light. "When did it happen?"

"When did what happen?" Nick asks gruffly.

"When did you stop looking at Kolter like your best friend, like your brother, like the best man you knew, and start looking at him like he's some vile monster? You and I both know everything you're saying isn't only not in his character, it's ridiculous."

Nick is quiet for a moment. "When did it happen?" he repeats.

I wait for him to continue.

"It happened the moment I found out he was fucking *our* little sister."

The call goes dead, and I let out a scream of frustration as I slam my fist down on the wheel.

The light turns green, so I have no choice but to keep driving.

He's so ridiculous. He doesn't even know what he's saying. He's not using logic; he's not listening. He's purely emotional, and I can't reason with someone like that.

There's a right turn coming up, so I move over to that lane and hit my blinker, noticing that the black SUV behind me does the same. Frowning, I study it in my rearview mirror. The windshield is blacked out—all the windows are actually—so I can't see the driver.

I'm supposed to take a left now, but something in me thinks better of it. Instead, I merge onto the freeway, heading in the opposite direction to my house.

The SUV does the same.

I sit up a little higher, and when I get the chance, I take a gap, jumping across all the freeway lanes to the very left. But the SUV does the same, maneuvering easily so it's right behind me once more.

My stomach turns and my heart begins hammering in my chest. I'm making this up. It has to be just a coincidence.

I hit my blinker then merge two lanes to the right, and for a moment, I think that's the end of it. Until the SUV takes a gap and is right behind me once more.

Fear seizes me, and I quickly dial Kolter. The phone rings twice as I sit there drumming my fingers on the steering wheel, my gaze bouncing between the road and my rearview mirror until he answers.

"Hey, Peaches. I can't talk right now. I'll call you—"

"I think I'm being followed," I cut in.

The phone goes quiet, and for a moment I think I've lost him.

"What do you mean?"

"I don't know. I was driving back to Mom's, and then I noticed this SUV was following me. So I got on the freeway and switched lanes, but he kept getting right behind me. I don't know if I accidently cut him off. I was on the phone with Nick, and I was distracted. Maybe I did. I just—"

"Shh, shh, deep breaths, Peaches. I need you to slow down and focus, alright?" Kolter says, cutting off my rambling.

The line sounds a little muffled before a motorcycle fires up in the background.

"Okay, where are you right this second?"

"I-I'm on I-5. Coming up to exit 162."

"Okay, what lane are you in?" Kolter asks, the sound of his motorcycle revving echoing in the background.

"Second to the far right," I say, looking in the mirror again.

"Take the exit. Quick," he instructs.

Without indicating, I whip the wheel hard, taking the exit at the very last minute. I watch my rearview mirror closely, and when I see the SUV do the same, full-on terror takes hold of me.

"No," I say nervously.

"What's happening, Peaches?"

"He got off too. Where do I go? What do I do?"

"Listen to me," he says. "They know that you see them. Just keep as much distance as you can. I've got your location. I'm two minutes out. Just hang a right and go straight."

I nod to myself and do as he says.

"Wait, how do you have my location? We've never shared locations before?"

He scoffs. "Like I'm not going to know where my girl is at all times?"

"Creepy and kinda sweet," I mutter, attempting to lighten the terrifying mood.

Kolter doesn't laugh at my joke and, honestly, fair—I'm not laughing either.

I take a right, and the SUV does as well, but they seem to be done with the chase because they speed up and slam into the back of me. I let out a scream, but I tighten my grip on the wheel and try to drive faster.

"What's happening?" Kolter shouts.

"They just hit me from behind!"

"They want you to pull over. DO NOT—you hear me? Keep driving."

I'm about to agree, but they hit me again and again, forcing a whimper out of me.

"I'm so scared," I choke out.

"I know, baby. I'm coming up. Keep going straight."

The SUV takes the shoulder then, speeding up before hitting the side of my car, sending me spinning into the middle of the road. All I can do is scream and hold on to the wheel for dear life. The car skids for several feet before I slam into a lamp post.

"Kolter?" I ask in a daze.

He doesn't respond, though.

I lift my head and look around to get my bearings.

A motorcycle comes peeling towards me, bullets flying past my car and hitting the SUV. They don't go through the glass, though, just pepper it with indents. Bulletproof glass? Who the heck are these people?

The SUV's doors open, and its passengers begin shooting at Kolter. He quickly pulls over, dumping his bike and ducking in front of my car as he returns fire. I lower myself in my seat as far as I can while still being able to watch everything that's happening.

Kolter tosses his gun to the side and begins firing another one as men in black suits emerge from the SUV, one advancing towards Kolter while another comes to the side of my car. Quickly, I look around for anything I can use as a weapon and find a miniature can of hairspray.

As soon as my door is ripped open, I mace the guy with the extra-hold can. He jolts in surprise, dropping his gun and clutching his face. I take that moment to kick him in the balls as hard as I can—because that drops any guy, right? When he tumbles to the ground, I grab my phone then jump out of the car and over him. But I soon realize my mistake. Now I'm out in the open in the middle of a shootout.

To my left, there are two men in suits sprawled on the ground, bullets between their eyes, and one more still standing, with his gun pointed at—

"Oh shit," I mutter as the man fires.

Someone throws themselves in front of me, but I don't piece together it's Kolter until I see the back of his leather jacket. He shoots a round of his own, dropping the guy and killing him instantly. Then Kolter wavers for a moment before dropping to the ground.

In a panic, I fall to my knees beside him, hauling his shirt up to find that he's been shot through the chest.

"Oh my God! Oh my God. You've been shot! I need to call 911," I say, scrabbling for my phone.

"No! *No!*" he says, grabbing me roughly, the pain evident on his face.

"Get me b-back to the club, Peaches. Can you do that?"

"What? You're shot! You need a hospital! I'm calling them."

He's lost his mind. He's in shock.

Kolter grabs my arm, his grip almost painful as he looks me in the eye.

"We can't go to the hospital, baby. Get me to the club."

I frown at him, but after a quick glance around the massacre, I nod and help him stand, so he can start limping towards the car.

Of course, the hairspray and brutal kick to the balls wasn't going to keep my attacker down for long. He's on his feet now and charging towards us—but Kolter just casually lifts the gun still in his hand and empties the clip into the man. He stumbles backward in shock before collapsing in the middle of the street.

My eyes are wide with shock as I open the back door of my car and shove Kolter inside. He's moaning in pain and writhing on his back, attempting to keep pressure on his chest.

"You know, being with you means having to be okay with a lot of murder," I huff.

Kolter lets out a rough chuckle that sends him into a coughing fit. Miraculously, my car still works, so I punch the gas and speed down the road.

"You're gonna be okay. I'm gonna get you there. Will they have everything to fix you?" I ask as I pull up the directions to the clubhouse.

"Call Ace—he'll have them ready," Kolter rasps.

"I don't have his number!" I shout in a panic, my eyes bouncing from the road to him and back again.

"Yes you do."

Frowning, I scroll through my contacts and find Ace almost immediately.

"You're so creepy," I mutter before hitting *call*.

The phone rings only once before a deep voice answers.

"Naomi? Is everything okay?"

"Kolter's been shot! Or Blade, or whatever! He won't let me take him to the hospital or call an ambulance, so I'm coming to the club."

Some muffled conversations occur in the background, then Ace is back.

"The doc is on his way. How bad is it?"

I look to the back of the car. Kolter's face is growing paler by the moment and blood is still pouring from his chest.

"Bad."

As soon as I pull up to the club, a rush of people swarm my car. The back door is ripped open, then several men grab Kolter and rush him inside. Ace stands by my door and helps me out, looking me over for injuries.

"You good?" he asks.

I nod, but I can't speak, the adrenaline finally waning. When I burst into tears. Ace quickly pushes my head to his chest, shielding me from everyone around.

"Hey, hey. It's okay. He's tough as nails—you know that. He's not going anywhere," he says softly.

I look up at him. "You can honestly promise that?"

Ace swallows roughly and tucks me tighter into his chest. "That bastard loves you too much to leave you. He'd fight the devil himself to be with you. It's gonna be okay."

I let out a choked sob as I nod, hoping, pleading, praying that he's right.

Two motorcycles pull up then, each rider leaping off before the bikes fully stop.

"What the fuck happened?" Matthew snarls and tears up the stairs, clearly not seeing Ace or me.

But Bones does. He follows Matthew for a moment before pausing and turning to us. Slowly, he stalks forward, his gaze roaming over my battered car, blood-soaked backseat and, well, the mess that I am.

"What happened?" he rumbles.

"Some men were following me. I don't know why. Kolter came and intercepted them. He got shot."

"Is he dead?" Bones asks stoically.

My eyes widen in outrage. "No!"

At least. I don't think... oh my God.

"Are they dead?" he asks.

I nod.

"How many?"

"Four, I think. I-I saw four bodies."

He lets out a heavy sigh that sounds more like a growl and rakes his hands through his hair. "Ace, you're with me. Grab a few more."

Ace hesitates for a moment, looking towards the clubhouse then back to me. "I think I should stay."

Bones has started walking away but slowly turns on his heel and gives him a death glare that chills me to the bone.

"I don't give a fuck what you think. You're with me. NOW."

Grudgingly, Ace steps away from me, gesturing for a few guys to follow as he mounts his bike.

"Where did this happen?" Bones asks, not looking up.

"I-I don't remember. I got off at 162 southbound. Took a right and went straight for a mile or two. I'm sorry."

His head whips up, his brows pinching like he's never heard the word *sorry*—like he doesn't understand its purpose. Then he fires up his own bike and backs it up before taking off down the road. Ace and two other bikers follow him, and I'm left standing in the parking lot... alone.

I'm only alone for a moment, though.

Matthew comes striding out the clubhouse door and makes a beeline for me. I don't attempt to hide how I shrink away from him, and he puts his hands up in surrender.

"You get hurt?" he asks.

I shake my head.

"Good."

We stand there in silence for a moment before I gather the courage to ask a question I'm not sure I want the answer to.

"H-How is he?"

Matthew's expression is stony. "Doc's doing everything he can for him. Won't know much for a bit."

An exhale escapes me as I stare down at the ground—and then the dam breaks, and I'm sobbing and shaking uncontrollably.

Matthew presses a heavy hand against my back, slowly rubbing up and down. I know it's supposed to be comforting, but something about him makes that impossible, though I suppose the effort is nice.

"I should have called 911. I should have gotten him an ambulance instead of driving him back here," I whisper.

"Why do you say that?" Matthew asks.

I look at him like he's crazy. "Because he's dying! He needs medical help, a hospital! The stubborn bastard wouldn't let me call them. It saved his life last time, though! God, I never thought... I never wanted to see him hurt like that again."

Matthew is quiet for a moment or two, his hand still rubbing my back. "Again?"

I look up at him, blinking away my tears, and sniff, "When he got shot at that warehouse years ago. He insisted I didn't call anyone then, but it saved his life. I just... if it wasn't for me, he wouldn't be hurt. And if I hadn't listened to him, he'd be at the hospital right now."

"You called the ambulance last time?" Matthew asks, a sharpness to his words that catches me off guard.

I nod.

He swallows roughly, then pulls out a cigarette and lights it. He takes a long inhale before blowing out the smoke. "He's a tough kid. He'll be fine."

Chapter Twenty Six
Kolter

I try to open my eyes, but my eyelids feel so heavy. Christ. My chest hurts like a motherfucker. Did I wipe out last night?

What's the last thing I remember? I rack my mind, but it's a total blank. I feel hungover, like I got into a fight and lost bad.

A soft voice echoes from a distance, and I do my best to focus on it. The more I do, the clearer it becomes until I can make out every single word.

"Kolter? Kolt, can you hear me?" she asks.

"Peaches," I murmur as the fog begins to lift.

I finally manage to open my eyes, and I'm confused to find myself in my bunk room at the clubhouse. I'm even more confused to see Naomi sitting in a chair beside me with bloodshot eyes and tear-soaked cheeks. Instantly, I'm on edge and push myself to sit up—or at least I try to. A sharp pain rips through me, and I wince and grip my chest.

What the fuck happened?

"Are you okay?" Naomi asks, her face filled with concern.

I take a few deep breaths, attempting to collect my thoughts—and then everything comes rushing back. Her phone call. The shootout.

Searing-hot pain ripping through me. My sight slowly fading, sounds turning muffled until there was just... nothing.

"I'm fine. Are you okay?" I ask, my gaze moving over her carefully.

She nods. "I'm fine. I was so worried about you. I thought I lost you," she chokes out.

I shake my head, pulling her towards me despite the pain that burns through me. "Shh, hey. I'm fine. I'm here. I'll never leave your side, Peaches. You're gonna have to throw a hell of a lot more than that my way to get rid of me."

Naomi lets out a choked laugh that sounds completely miserable. I hate seeing her like this, and I do my best to wipe her tears away as fast as they fall.

"What happened? Was everything... cleaned up?" I ask carefully.

Naomi nods. "Ace and Bones went out there and, I don't know, did whatever they needed to. They came back and told Matthew it was sorted."

I nod. Good—that's good. The last thing we need on top of everything else is an investigation, though I can't believe no one called the cops given all that gunfire. Maybe they were just slow to arrive, and Bones and Ace beat them there.

"He's been nice enough?" I ask, alluding to my father.

Naomi needs no explanation. Instead, she nods. "Actually, he's been really kind. He was worried about you."

My brows furrow in disbelief, but I don't argue. Instead, I wrap my arms around her tighter, pressing her to me so I never forget what it feels like. Fuck, it's been a while since I came that close to death. It's humbling, awakening and makes me grateful for everything I have. Every moment, every second with her is a blessing I don't intend on wasting.

When Naomi helps me up, she asks me what I need. Truthfully, the only thing I want is to get the hell out of here. I know why those guys followed her, I know why they chose to target her and I know exactly who ordered it.

The mafia doesn't take kindly to betrayal, let alone theft, and that's exactly what we did. Thanks to my father, we stole from them —stole their shipment right in front of their faces and were then forced to kill them to survive it.

Of course they followed me after that. Probably followed a lot of us. They followed, they watched and they found my weakness. Fuck if they didn't almost take her away too. I'm not sure she realizes how close to death she really was. She's too focused on me; she's missed the bigger picture. Her involvement with me has put her life in danger, and as selfish as I want to be with her, I can't help but feel like I have to let her go.

The instant those big, beautiful eyes land on me, though, that plan is obliterated into a million pieces. I can't live without her, not anymore. Not ever again. Even if that means we both fall from my selfishness, at least we'll have one another. Forever.

I'm surprised to find my father seemingly waiting outside my room. Even more surprised when he says I should take a few days of rest away from the club. I should be relieved, but I just feel on edge. Trauma, I suppose. I'm conditioned to only expect the worst from him, after all.

It does catch me off guard how morose he seems. He apologizes for making the choices that led to this, though he doesn't go into further detail in front of Naomi. He doesn't need to, though. I understand what he means, and I'm fucking shocked.

He doesn't say anything beyond that. He just nods at the two of us and heads into the back. Bones follows him a moment later, clapping my shoulder on the way past—his version of, *I'm glad you didn't die, kid.*

I don't hesitate a moment longer, despite the growing crowd of people who begin asking me questions, checking in or wanting details. Instead of acknowledging any of them, I take Naomi's hand in mine, and we head out the front door.

Naomi drives us home in her car, her expression turning pained whenever her gaze is drawn to the dried blood on the backseat. My dried blood.

Guilt continues gnawing at me the entire way back. I want out. Out of this club, out of this life. I want to throw Naomi over my shoulder and disappear into the night, never to be seen again. Once it was safe enough, we'd contact Mom and Anthony and Nick. Until then, it would just be us. Alone. Safe. Free.

That's a fantasy, though. It's not how this world works. Blood in, blood out—you ride together, or you end up six feet under. That's just the reality, a reality I knew when I became a member, though if I'm honest, it wasn't a path I fully chose for myself. I sure as hell wouldn't have chosen it, no matter the circumstances, knowing what I do now; having what I do now.

When we step into my apartment, Naomi is quick to tend to me, holding the door open, taking my shoes off for me and softly guiding me towards the couch. I know she's just trying to help, but I hate it. It makes me feel weak, useless. I don't want her to look at me like I'm some wounded baby bird.

She moves to step away once I'm seated on the couch, but I grab her wrist and tug her towards me. Naomi stumbles forward, failing to catch herself, which works out perfectly for me. She lands in my lap, and I grunt in discomfort from being jostled before I grip her hips, pinning her into place perfectly.

"Kolter, stop! I'm going to hurt you," she complains, trying to wiggle away from me.

"I'm fine, Peaches. Look at me. Picture of health," I say, glancing down at myself.

She rolls her eyes like she doesn't buy my shit for a moment before trying to stand up once more. I hold her tighter, ensuring she can't move an inch, and she lets out a frustrated huff.

"Why are you so stubborn? You don't have to be tough all the time. You're hurt—let me take care of you," she says gently.

Her sweet voice tugs at my heart, and I lift my head up to meet hers, brushing my lips against her own. She's resistant for only a moment before her mouth gives way to me, softly moving in rhythm with mine before her tongue swipes in.

"You are taking care of me, baby. Let me take care of you," I murmur against her lips.

She scoffs and shakes her head, though she's smiling. "You really think I'm going to let you have sex with me when you literally almost died yesterday?"

I trace my thumbs over the exposed skin where the hem of her shirt has ridden up, then pull away so I can look at her fully. "Maybe not, but I think we both need this."

"Why?" she asks, amusement lacing her tone.

"Because you need the reminder that I'm still here, and I need the reminder that you're not going anywhere."

She softens then, her brows knitting together as a clouded look enters her eyes—and then she nods.

She grips the bottom of her shirt, tugs it over her head and tosses it to the floor, then stands, her hands moving to the button of her jeans. Slowly, she unfastens them and peels them down her legs. My cock jerks in response, and I palm it through my sweatpants, stroking it slowly as I watch her.

"Take off the bra next," I rasp and slip my hand into my sweats so I can grip my cock fully.

She reaches behind her back, freeing the clasp and allowing her breasts to spill out.

Fuck.

My hand moves faster, and a bead of pre-cum spreads from my tip.

I watch with rapt attention as Naomi skates a hand down her chest, past her stomach and pauses at her panties. I think my shy girl is nervous, and I'm ready to encourage her to keep going, but then she pushes her hand beneath the lacy material and slips a finger inside herself.

A pleasured gasp escapes her that turns my breathing labored.

"That feel good?" I choke out.

She nods, her eyes dilated as they meet mine. Then she sinks her teeth into her lower lip and pushes a second finger inside.

"Oh my gosh, Kolt," she whimpers.

"That's right, Peaches. Pretend it's my fingers inside you right now. What would I do next?" I ask, my movements on my cock turning jerky.

She pulls her panties down with her other hand, gifting me the beautiful sight of her before that hand moves to her clit. It's swollen and practically begging for attention.

As soon as her fingertips touch it, her entire body shudders. She's standing over me like a moaning goddess, and I'm a mere mortal on his knees for her.

"That's my perfect girl. You're doing beautifully," I encourage.

"L-Let me see you," she stutters before another soft moan escapes her.

I don't hesitate, moving a little faster than I should, but I ignore the punishing twinge of pain and push my sweats down my legs, allowing her to watch me as I stroke my cock to the sight of her.

Her mouth parts in what looks like desire as her hand quickens against her clit.

"Kolter, I'm gonna—I'm gonna—Oh god," she cries out.

I know she's moments from falling apart, and I'm all for playing, but there's only one place I want her coming.

I reach forward and yank her towards me once more, and this time she falls much more willingly, her legs either side of my lap. I take full advantage and thrust my cock right between her thighs.

Her back arches, her head dropping back as her orgasm slams into her. That's all it took. A little teasing, one deep thrust and fucking fireworks. That's how it always is with her. Like goddamn magic.

"That's good, Peaches. Just like that. You only ever come on my cock or my tongue. Is that clear?" I grunt as I continue fucking her hard and rough.

She gasps and moans, nodding shakily as she rides wave after wave of her pleasure.

I feel my own release beginning to build, and I don't want to hold off any longer.

"Kiss me," I grit through clenched teeth as I begin losing any composure.

I feel her lips on me in the next moment, and that's all I need to completely lose it. My orgasm hits me like a fucking freight train, my cock throbbing my cum into her, showing no sign of stopping as our tongues and moans meld together in a perfect storm.

When we've wrung every possible ounce of pleasure out of one another, we collapse into each other, our sweat-coated skin sticking together as our heavy breathing gradually evens out. For a moment, I think she might even have fallen asleep, but then her soft voice rasps against my chest.

"I'll never go anywhere, Kolter. You never have to worry about that. No matter what we have to go through, it's worth it to share this life with you."

Her head lifts and her eyes gaze into mine as my chest tightens with love and sorrow.

I'm blessed beyond belief to have earned a love like this from a woman like her. Even more so given she can look in on some of my worst days and love me all the same. But I'm filled with sorrow at the idea that this is all our life will ever be. Danger, tragedy, fear. I don't want that for her. She deserves more—better. I just have to come up with a plan so I can give that to her.

And fast.

Chapter Twenty Seven
Naomi

I've pretty much been attached to Kolter's hip for the last two days —I've barely let him pee without me. He tries to act tough, like he doesn't need anything, but he almost died. The doctor said he was very touch and go, so rest is the most important part of his recovery. I've been doing what I can, but he's made it impossible to fully watch over him, and now he's snuck out of the house while I was sleeping.

He sent me a text saying he was going to the store for provisions and would be back soon, but that was hours ago, and I'm getting impatient. I'm half tempted to go looking for him. I don't even know how he left the place, unless he took a rideshare or something, since his bike is still back at the club.

Ace has texted me a few times to check in on Kolter. Apparently, Kolter hasn't been responding to any of his messages. I mean, I kind of understand that. All we've been doing is eating, sleeping, and screwing, though we've had to get creative when it comes to that last one. Kolter insists he's fine, but I know him too well to believe a word out of his lying mouth.

I'm just responding to a message from Cassi when another text comes in.

Kolter: Meet me here as soon as you can.

Then a pin comes in, dropping the address of a little diner about forty minutes away in the middle of nowhere.

I frown as I text him back.

Me: Why? What's going on? Are you okay?

Kolter: More shit with the club. I need to get you somewhere safe. Don't bother grabbing anything. Just hurry, Peaches.

Anxiety fills me as I climb out of bed and slide on some clothes. Worst-case scenarios begin playing in my head, and when I try to call Kolter and it goes to voicemail, I really start to freak out.

I'm in the car in less than ten minutes, my fingers drumming nervously against the steering wheel as I follow Kolter's directions.

For a moment, I'm tempted to call Ace and see if he knows what's going on. I think better of it, though. I don't know what Kolter means when he says things with the club. I know he trusts Ace, and so do I, but I'm worried about putting him in danger if I let on that I know something I shouldn't.

I wish Kolter had picked a closer meet-up point so I'd have less time to spiral out of control.

When I finally pull into the parking lot, I blow out a breath, relieved to see Kolter's bike out front. There are only two other cars here—we must be the only people here besides the workers.

I step through the front door and look around the small diner. Matthew is sitting in one of the booths. For a moment, I'm not sure if he's supposed to see me, but when he makes eye contact and smiles, waving me over, I lower my guard a little.

What the heck is going on?

When I reach him, he gestures for me to take the seat across from him.

"What's going on?" I ask, looking around for any sight of Kolter.

"I feel like we haven't gotten to chat enough. Thanks for meeting me."

"Meeting you?" I ask.

I have no idea what's going on.

Matthew pulls Kolter's phone out of his pocket, dangling it between us before setting it on the table. Instantly, a ball of lead drops into my stomach, chills racing up and down my spine.

"W-Where is Kolter?"

"He's around," Matthew says cryptically.

"Around where?" I ask, attempting to keep my tone steady and firm.

Irritation fills Matthew's gaze before he whistles.

The doors leading to what I assume is the kitchen open, and Bones drags out a bleeding Kolter.

"Oh my God," I gasp, rising from my seat.

Matthew's hand shoots out like a striking viper, gripping my arm and pinning me in place.

"You will stay seated until you're excused. It's bad manners otherwise."

Kolter's head lolls forward, blood dripping down his face from his eyebrow. His gaze is confused, unfocused—until he sees me. It seems that's all he needs to rouse himself, and he rears against Bones' grip, attempting to reach me, but Bones easily holds him back.

"No! Fuck. What are you doing?" he spits at his father.

"While you were bleeding to death in the back of the club, your little girlfriend and I had an interesting chat," Matthew says.

My brows knit together in confusion.

"Something about her being the one that called the ambulance the knight the mafia gunned you down on Rainier."

Panic fills Kolter's eyes, and he quickly shakes his head. "She didn't. I did. I was fading and got scared and called for help. I told you that," Kolter lies.

"That's what I believed for years, and I nearly killed you for it then. The ambulance found you alright—as did the police, who seized three million dollars worth of merchandise from our warehouse. If it wasn't for Slinky taking the fall for ownership, I'd have been right back behind bars again. Still would be, in fact. That's a pretty costly mistake, but I was willing to forgive it. Especially after all the years of dedication you've offered me and the club," Matthew says.

His gaze turns to me then, his grip on my arm still punishing, and his tone takes on a sharp edge. "But then this little slice of pie shows up out of nowhere all these years later, and all of a sudden, you're not coming to meetings, you're cutting out of duties. You're impossible to track down, and when the boys do find you, where are you? Always with this one."

I look to Kolter, but his gaze is fully focused on his father.

"I didn't like how weak she was making you," Matthew continues. "She was a distraction, one that would have to go eventually. Then I started to convince myself she could be useful. Once I found out her fat mouth caused one of the largest losses our club has faced, though? It confirmed every doubt I had about her," he says, pulling a gun out from under the table and aiming it right at me.

"No," Kolter snarls, stomping on Bones' foot before elbowing him in the face and breaking free.

I take advantage of the moment, surging to my feet when Matthew's hold on me loosens.

Kolter charges for his dad, but Matthew's already standing and punches him in the chest—right where he was shot—before smacking him across the face with his gun. Kolter drops to the ground, and Matthew turns to me, pointing the gun at me once more.

I lift my hands in the air, shaking uncontrollably. "P-Please. I-I'm sorry. I was just a kid. I didn't know. I was just trying to save h-him."

Matthew gives me a pitying look. "Shhh, don't cry, sweetheart. This isn't personal. I think you're a sweet girl. You've certainly grown into yourself well, and I'd be lying if I said I wasn't disappointed I won't get to see if you taste as good as your mother."

My stomach curls at his vile words, tears pouring down my face.

"I'd keep you around for myself if I could. Unfortunately, this isn't just business—it's a lesson," he says, glancing at Kolter, who's bleeding profusely on the ground, Bones' boot holding him in place.

"Say goodnight," he says, looking back at me.

A shot rings out, and I jolt, my eyes widening in horror as Kolter lets out a soul-crushing scream. Time slows, my brain struggling to catch up with my eyes, and a body thuds to the floor.

Oh my God...

But it's Matthew, a huge hole blown through the side of his head, blood and brain matter splattered against the diner window. I wait for him to get up, to come for me or Kolter, but he doesn't—he just lies there, creating a larger and larger puddle of blood.

He's dead.

He's dead.

Wait. Who—?

Everything is still moving in slow motion, and it takes my mind entirely too long to process the scene before me. Then I see it. The gun in Bones' hand, still aimed where Matthew once stood. His eyes meet mine, but that gut-clenching fear doesn't dissipate until he lifts his foot and releases Kolter, his gaze still firmly on me.

Kolter scrambles towards me, cupping my face in his hands as a tear skates down his cheek. "I'm so sorry, Peaches."

The sound of a throat clearing jolts Kolter into action, and he turns round in a flash, shielding my body with his as he faces Bones.

"What are you playing at?"

"I'm not playing at anything," he says stiffly.

"You just killed your president... your best friend," Kolter says.

Bones nods once.

"Why?" I ask, stepping out from behind Kolter carefully.

Bones is still brandishing his gun, but I have a feeling if he wanted either of us dead, he wouldn't have intervened. Which begs the question...

"Why did you do it?"

His jaw tightens as he blows out a short breath through his nose. Silence stretches between us for several seconds, so long that I think he won't respond, and then he finally says:

"I wasn't gonna let him take out my kid."

Shock and confusion slam into me. His what?

Epilogue
Kolter

"I'm sorry, what?" I ask.

I couldn't have heard Bones right. His *kid*? Naomi? What the fuck?

"No," Naomi says softly, shaking her head. "M-My dad's name was Anthony. He left shortly after I was born, but he was definitely my dad, and my brothers'."

Bones levels Naomi with his typical blank stare, though I can see a small twinkle of emotion in his eyes as he clears his throat.

"Why do you think he took off? He stuck around for two kids, but three was too many?" he scoffs.

"You and my mom had an affair," Naomi guesses.

Bones nods. "Anthony was suspicious but didn't actually confront her until after you were born. Guess he got a paternity test done while you were in the hospital."

I blow out a breath and run a hand through my hair. I mean... I just don't even know what to say. This is fucking insane.

"Why didn't she ever tell me?" Naomi asks, echoing the disbelief I feel. "I mean, I'm sure she wasn't proud of cheating on her husband, but still. Didn't I have a right to know who my father was? Unless you asked her not to?"

Bones stays quiet for a moment, and a flash of hurt passes over her face.

"Must have been quite the nightmare for you when I showed up at the club one day." She laughs bitterly. "The kid you tried to forget, tried to ignore comes barging into your life one way or another. You can't write that stuff, huh?"

I expect Bones to stay quiet, so it surprises me when he says, "I wanted to know you."

We both look at him with furrowed brows.

And then the rigid, emotionless biker I've known my whole life stands up a little taller. "I asked your mom if I could meet you—a lot. Have a relationship with you. She wouldn't allow it. She didn't want this life to find you, and there was no backing out for me. I didn't want this life to find you either, so it was for the best."

His words seem to bring Naomi a semblance of peace, and she does something completely unexpected. She offers her hand to Bones. He looks down at it like he's inspecting it for ill intent before shaking it slowly.

"Thank you for telling me the truth and for saving my life, Bones," she says.

"Jerry," he rasps.

She gives him a tight smile. "Jerry."

Then she turns to me, and I wrap my arms around her, holding her close as I reflect on how close I was to losing her.

Bones watches us leave with a steady eye, though I don't miss the heavy wave of emotions that rushes over his face, especially when Naomi doesn't turn around once.

After word spreads that my father's no more, Bones quickly assumes control of the club. A few guys who were loyal to my father leave without a trace, but no one outright opposes him. In fact, the majority of them are relieved. No one was happy with the way he was running shit, so it seems a change in leadership is exactly what they needed. I also take the opportunity to do what I need.

I walk into the clubhouse, sit down and tell him straight up.

I want out.

He looks at me for a moment like he's waiting for the punchline. People don't just ask to get out. The guys that defect are barred and blacklisted, and if they ever show their faces in Seattle again... well, let's just say it's better they don't. Which is why me sitting down and asking politely to leave the MC must be a fucking joke.

I'm not playing, though.

I sit there in silence for what feels like hours before Bones finally gives me one terse nod. No parting words or gestures. No threats or favors. A simple release. Just like that, I'm free, and fuck if I don't feel like it too, like a thousand pounds has been lifted from my shoulders.

I. Am. Free.

When I tell Naomi I'm out of the club, she breaks down in tears. She knows it was never where I wanted to be, that it wasn't what I wanted for our life, and now we have a chance at a real, fully-fledged happily ever after. The whole fucking nine yards.

Nick comes by our apartment a few weeks after that, and when I open the door, I half expect him to pick up right where we left off. Instead, he gives me a sharp look and threatens to break my legs if I ever hurt her before storming away. It's the closest thing to a blessing we'll ever get from him, and it's good enough for both of us.

Even Bones—or Jerry, I guess—attempts to make amends.

One night, we're all at Mom's for family dinner when there's a knock at the door. She goes to answer it and freezes in place when she sees the mountain of a man standing in the doorway, looking almost nervous. His beard is combed, his jeans are clean and he has a small bouquet of wildflowers clenched in his meaty fist.

I half expect her to slam the door in his face but instead, tears well up in her eyes and she throws herself into his arms. He holds her tight, like she's the most precious thing in the world, and it honestly takes us all by surprise.

Mom invites him in, and after that, he doesn't miss a family dinner once. No one questions his presence; no one asks what their relationship is. Honestly, you'd hardly even know he was there, except for the fact he's a 250-pound biker whose hand is permanently attached to Mom's leg.

Bones is also trying to build a relationship with Naomi. He asks her at every dinner if he can take her to breakfast the next day. She always declines, but he never stops trying. I gotta admit, I admire the hell out of his perseverance and his respect for her boundaries, so I secretly hope she gives him a chance one day. I've known the guy my whole life, and he's not perfect by any means, and probably not the type of guy she'd ever have pictured for her father, but he's a good man, and she could do a lot worse.

Trust me.

I feel no grief for my own father. We didn't hold a funeral or a celebration of life—there was nothing of his life worth celebrating. Bones buried him somewhere he'll never be found, and that's good enough for me. That piece of shit tried to snatch my entire world away just to prove a point, to keep me in line. I'm just sorry I didn't kill the fucker myself.

<hr>

We're currently packing for a summer backpacking trip across Europe, now Naomi's got her bachelor's degree. Neither of us have been, and we're both more than eager to get away from... well, everything.

She looks up at me over her suitcase, delivering a sweet smile that almost brings me to my knees. I toss my socks to the side, lean over the bed and cup the nape of her neck, so her lips press against my own. Our tongues tangle together as we sink into one another, complete euphoria that only she can bring washing over me.

The best is yet to come—I know that for certain. We can do anything, be anyone, and I'll happily let her pave our way. By her side is where I'm meant to be.

By her side, I know I'm finally home.

Extended Epilogue
Naomi

We're leaving for Europe in two days, and I couldn't be more excited. We're starting in London before moving on to Paris, Venice, Munich and then who knows? I've decided to put a hold on school now that I have my bachelor's degree; besides, where better to get raw journalistic experience than on the road? Mom doesn't like the idea of us running wild in Europe, but I remind her that it's safer than her spending most every night in bed with the president of a motorcycle club. That tends to silence her fairly quickly.

I've adjusted to the idea that Anthony Sr isn't my real father; that Jerry is. It makes sense now that he left, and Mom was obviously in the wrong for having an affair.

She and I sat down and talked about everything that happened back then. How she grew up with Jerry and Matthew. How she would hang out at the club before she had any of us. How she and Jerry quickly fell in love, and how he pushed her away when things got too dangerous.

Then she met Anthony Sr, they got married, had Anthony and Nick, and then... she and Jerry reconnected. It was like no time had passed. She hated the sneaking around and the lying, but she would never and could never expose her kids to the club's lifestyle. So they ended things again, and I was a parting gift of sorts.

Anthony had felt Mom pulling away and had suspicions about my paternity, since they were rarely intimate during that time. And when it was confirmed he wasn't my father, he just packed up and left.

I get not wanting to have anything to do with me and Mom, but the boys? They deserved better.

Jerry seems to be a pretty decent man honestly. I already had a good opinion of him, from the stories Kolter's told me about his childhood, plus the whole saving-my-life thing. But he makes my mom so happy, happier than I've ever seen her in my life, and that is worth everything.

I know I'm probably being too harsh, rejecting him constantly. I should give him a chance, give us both a chance to form... I don't know, some kind of a relationship. And I will. Someday. Maybe.

I do my best to push all of that away for now. Tonight is girls' night, the last one we'll get for quite some time.

Arianna's bump is growing by the day, and she's due in less than three months. I already told Kolter that when it gets close to her due date, we're flying back. There's no way I'm missing out on my best friend's baby for anything.

Arianna and Logan eloped, which Cassi and I incessantly give her crap for, because how could she not invite us to the wedding? They wanted it to be simple and intimate, and honestly that's perfect for them. We all know that Cassi's wedding will be none of those things, so we'll be able to celebrate enough for both couples.

Nico proposed in the most dramatic way possible—perfect for Cassi. He filled an entire restaurant with roses and candles and hired a string quartet to play beneath a huge heart lit up with the words "Will you marry me?" He also hired a videographer to capture every moment, and when I tell you Cassi bawled like a baby, I'm not exaggerating in the slightest.

Since then, she references her *fiancé*, the wedding or some other wedding-related event in every other conversation, and it makes me smile every time. Each of my friends deserve the world, and it seems they've both landed men who're willing to give it to them.

Kolter has asked me several times if I want to take that next step with him. I mean, honestly, it's a stupid question. Of course I do, but also, I don't feel the need to rush things. I don't need a ring to prove that he's mine or I'm his. We've belonged to each other since the moment we met. A legal document from the state isn't going to change that.

For now, we're enjoying our quiet, peaceful life, content to celebrate our friends' happiness, but when the time is right, we will absolutely throw the party of a lifetime, where I'll do my absolute best to soak up every moment while staying out of the spotlight as much as possible. Wish me luck on that.

"I can't believe you're going on a backpacking trip through Europe with Kolter. Like, is anyone else having a hard time wrapping their head around the fact that our sweet little Nay bae is dating her brother? I'm just so proud," Cassi teases.

I roll my eyes and toss a dinner roll at her—thankfully, we decided to order room service instead of eating out—and she laughs.

"Says the woman who's engaged to her sister's ex-boyfriend," Arianna says before taking a huge bite of chocolate cake.

"Coming from the woman who's married to her ex-stepfather and pregnant with his baby," I point out.

Arianna swallows the cake and throws me an outraged look. "Hey! I was standing up for you, bitch."

We all laugh, then Cassi shakes her head.

"We are kind of a fucked-up bunch, huh? Like, imagine the movies they could make about our lives."

I shrug. "I'd watch them."

Arianna nods. "Too bad it would never happen. Logan and I have kinky sex way too often."

Cassi snaps her fingers in response, then we dissolve into fits of laughter.

"I'm going to miss you guys," I sigh.

"Us too, babe," Arianna says.

"But we'll all get together soon for our sweet baby niece," Cassi says, rubbing Arianna's belly lovingly.

Ari rolls her eyes. "I told you we aren't finding out what the baby is until it's born."

Cassi waves her off like the comment is irrelevant. "I'm manifesting—leave me alone, okay?"

Ari shakes her head and finishes her cake before pushing the plethora of room service plates away from us.

"Alright, notification check—what do you ladies got?" Cassi asks as she scrolls through her phone.

"I have one missed call, two text messages and a random reel," Arianna says.

Cassi laughs. "I'll raise your missed call with two and three text messages."

I pull out my phone and shake my head. "Three missed calls, one missed FaceTime, two text messages and a voicemail demanding to know if I'm okay."

The girls laugh.

"Okay, surprise, surprise—Naomi wins most overbearing spouse for the night."

"Lucky me," I scoff.

"I mean, to be fair, your man was literally a criminal. He's used to no answer meaning someone's dead," Arianna points out.

"Criminal is harsh," I say.

"But true," Cassi cuts in.

They actually love Kolter—they always have, ever since we were kids. After I told them everything that happened—from the mafia trying to take us out to his own father pulling a gun on me—they've adopted this theory that Kolter is a hardened criminal. Which, I guess when he needs to be, sure.

Cassi perks up, a wicked smile spreading over her face as she looks around the room. "I have an idea."

She quickly types out a text, then shows it to us before sending in. Arianna and I smile and send the same text to our guys before we get up and get dressed.

We're going out tonight. Maybe to a club or something like it. You can meet us if you want.

In less than an hour, we're dressed and standing inside the main entrance of the sex club where all this began. A rush of familiarity hits me, and yet everything feels different.

As if the guys were all together already, they pile into the club as one, quickly scanning the room before their eyes land on us.

Logan wraps his arm around Arianna and yanks her into a kiss before leading her upstairs, while Nico lifts Cassi up and hauls her off in the other direction. Kolter, though? He stalks towards me like he has all the time in the world. Like I'd wait a hundred lifetimes for him.

Probably because I would.

When he reaches me, he pulls me close, claiming me for all to see before pulling away.

"You think you can just walk into my club anytime you feel like it without me by your side?" he rumbles.

A smile tugs at my mouth as I loop my arms around his neck. "What's yours is mine, right?"

I grind myself against him, and he lets out a groan as his hold on me turns punishing.

"You've got that fucking right, Peaches."

Without a single warning, Kolter scoops me up into his arms and begins carrying me away. I can't help but giggle as he climbs the stairs, pushing us into the first room available before locking the door.

It's crazy to think how much has changed. How much we've been through. How different we've all become. How everything started here.

One moment.

One touch.

One night.

Thank You

Phew, and there you have it, the final story in the *One Night* series! If these characters can promise anything, it's a quick, fun, spicy read that leaves you questioning if it's you or society that has it all wrong!

If you haven't read the first two books and want to know more about Arianna and Cassi's stories, check them out here!

Grab *One Night Seduction* here! (Arianna's story)
Grab *One Night Scandal* here! (Cassi's story)

If you're looking for your next read, then look no further. Angsty, emotional, forbidden love with a scorching amount of spice is at your service below!

Locked In: Season One—a reality TV romance meets thriller

The Gallows Hill Series—a dark academia reverse harem
Deceit
Descent
Demise

Damnation—prequel (Though I suggest reading after!)

The Alphaletes Series—interconnected football romance stories
    The Loyalties We Break
    The Walls We Break
    The Hearts We Break
    The Rules We Break

Standalones
    Deliverance—an FF forbidden romance
    Gratify—a forbidden age gap
    Graves—an MFM stalker romance
    Jagged Harts—an MMA enemies to lovers
    Graves & Griggs: A Very Bloody Christmas (novella crossover of
Gallows Hill Trilogy x **Graves**)